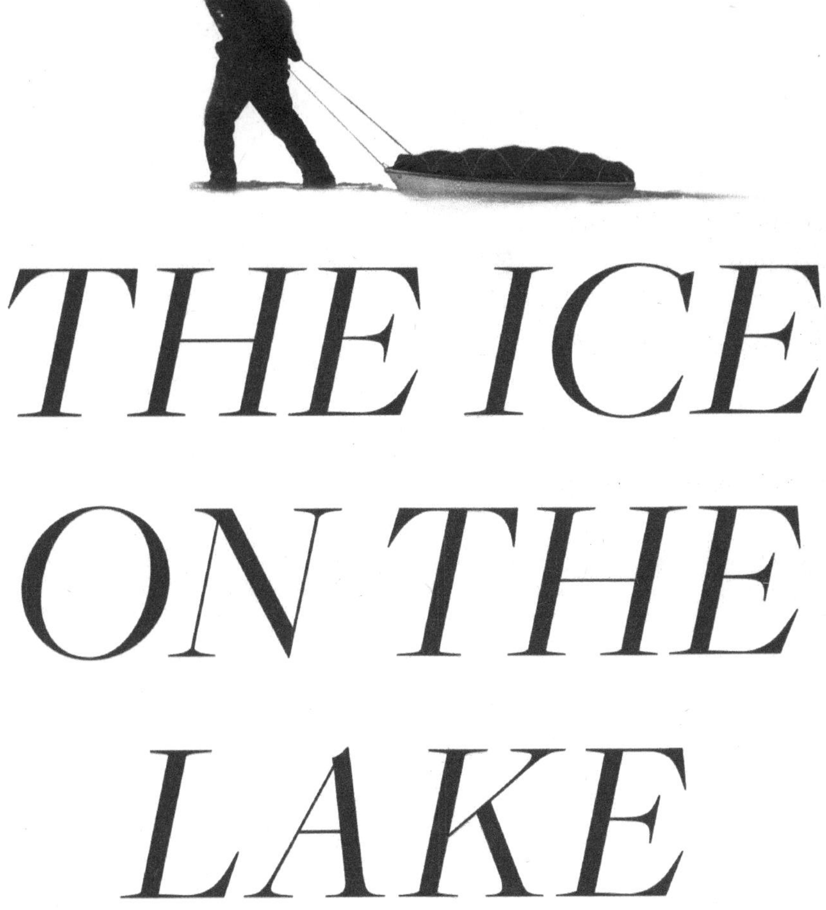

THE ICE ON THE LAKE

BOOKS BY ALEX MESSENGER

FICTION

The Ice on the Lake

NONFICTION

The Twenty-Ninth Day: Surviving a Grizzly Attack in the Canadian Tundra

ALEX MESSENGER

THE ICE ON THE LAKE

Published in 2026 by Blackstone Publishing
Cover and book design by Alenka Linaschke

Printed in the United States of America

First edition: 2026
ISBN 979-8-228-30009-5
Fiction / Thrillers / Suspense

Version 1

Blackstone Publishing
31 Mistletoe Rd.
Ashland, OR 97520

www.BlackstonePublishing.com

Dedicated to those who find the missing, care for the injured,
and respectfully recover the dead.

PART I

CHAPTER ONE

The last time Hugh saw his wife was on a Tuesday.

It had been cold, maybe five degrees, when the sun dipped below the horizon a few hours before. It would be colder now, but that was typical for January in Duluth. It was dark and clear, a sliver of moon rising from behind the earth. They were home, but she was going out, off to a friend's house. He could still see Sarah in a blink of memory. We never dwell too much on the mundane until there's a reason to, something to mark a moment as auspicious or foreboding, the end of normal. He had been watching the empty doorway when she leaned back in to lift a ring of keys off a hook on the wall. Her purse dangled from a shoulder. She adjusted her green wool scarf and salt-and-pepper hat. "Okay, I think that's it," she said. "Are you all good?"

Hugh looked back to a spoon he was holding out for his son. Jason's dexterity and coordination at one year old ruled out a tidy meal, but they were trying with some pea soup. Most of it was on his face, but enough had made it into his mouth that he realized he loved it.

"Yeah," Hugh said, wiping a streak of green from near Jason's eye. "We're all good here."

Their daughter, Lauren, was sitting in the living room, absorbed in a book about a cuddly bear and his forest friends on a quest for honey. She threw the book aside and jumped up, running to the door.

"Bye, Mommy," she said, arms up. Sarah bent down and picked the girl up, wrapping her in a tight hug.

"Bye, sweetheart," she said, and leaned back to plant a big kiss on her cheek. "You have a fun night with Daddy, and I'll see you in the morning."

She looked over at Hugh, and he smiled. Sarah set the girl down, and she ran back to her book.

"Drive safe and have fun," Hugh said. A smile spread his dark beard and pinched crow's-feet at the corners of his eyes. "And don't rush home. We'll be getting to bed before long. We'll be all good here."

Sarah's eyes creased with a smile, and she blew a kiss across the room. "I'm off," she said. Then she ducked through the door out to the garage and their old Ford sedan. Hugh heard the engine turn over, and the garage door open, then close again.

He patted his son's head, straightening the soft blond hair over to one side. The boy ignored the touch, brows tensed on the task of eating, eyes focused somewhere beyond the bowl and the spoon. Hugh looked from his son to his daughter on the couch. The amber light from a floor lamp cast her in a cozy glow, the waves of her hair a golden halo. Across her lap, those well-worn pages. She knew the book from cover to cover and could recite the text in its entirety, despite her inability to read. Still, her eyes pored over the pages, examining each image as she played the words in her mind, before turning the page in earnest to see what happened next.

Hugh smiled, sat back in his chair, and breathed in the serene scene. It was the start of a normal night.

It would never happen again.

The next morning, Hugh woke early. He was surprised when he reached across the bed to find the sheets still crisply tucked, the comforter flat against the mattress. Her side was still empty. Cold. He padded downstairs, careful not to wake the kids, and found the couches empty. The car wasn't in the garage either.

Sarah hadn't come home. She'd probably had a bit too much to drink and decided to stay there instead of making the drive back on country roads. Still, it worried him. He leafed through the papers on the kitchen counter, looking for a reminder of where she'd been going, maybe a phone number. The papers weren't helpful, but then he remembered the calendar. Stupid not to think of it. It was covered in short summaries of their activities, short verses on their shared life like poetry. He thumbed the booklet off the wall and traced the dates. Yesterday said "dinner at Jena's" in Sarah's bold, swooping handwriting. Hugh didn't know Jena's number. Sarah kept a small binder in her purse with most of her friends' contact information, a little leather notebook with a pocket for papers. She'd have that with her, so Hugh pulled the big phone book from the cupboard. He laid the book on the counter, flipped past the yellow pages to the section for *L*. When he got to the right page, his finger traced the names until he found *Lindstrom* and Jena's house on Island Lake.

He went over to the wall-mounted phone and lifted the receiver, the drone of a dial tone audible through the small speaker. Back at the counter, his finger traced the digits on the page of newsprint, and he thumbed the corresponding buttons on the phone, the numbers glowing green in the dim morning light. He held the phone to his ear. It rang, and he subconsciously rubbed his hand across his forehead as if to erase the worry that was creasing there. After three rings, the bell stopped with a click, and he heard Jena's tired voice through the analog earpiece.

"Hello?"

"Hey, Jena, it's Hugh McLaren," he said. "I'm sorry to call you so early. I'm guessing you all had a late night, but I wanted to check to see if Sarah had spent the night there. She didn't come home, so I thought maybe she'd just decided to stay."

There was a long pause on the line before Jena spoke again. "No, Hugh, she didn't come last night," she said, her words awkward and heavy.

"What do you mean?" Hugh said.

"Well, she was supposed to come, but she never showed up," Jena said. "I figured something came up with you or the kids and she couldn't make it out. Is that . . . That's not it, huh?"

Hugh's throat had gone dry, and his stomach tensed like a coiling snake. He suddenly felt hot. His hand had stopped rubbing his forehead, and he was now pressing it firmly at his brow and cheekbone, willing understanding from his brain.

"No. No, she left last night," he said. "She left here and she was headed your way. I think it must have been six or six thirty. She never showed?"

"No. Like I said, we just thought she had to cancel last minute," Jena said. "I meant to call and check but didn't think about it again. I don't know what to say, Hugh . . ."

"Oh, god, I need to think," Hugh said. "Is there anyone on the way you think she might have stopped over to . . ."

A loud knock interrupted him. He startled, nearly dropping the phone, and turned to the front door, uncertain.

"Hold on, Jena, someone's at the door," Hugh said. "Maybe she got held up and lost her keys or something. I'll talk to you later." The knock came again.

But Sarah wouldn't knock.

He set the phone down on the cradle and left the kitchen. When he opened the door, he didn't find his wife. He was met by a man dressed head to toe in brown, a sparkle of gold from the badge on his breast.

"Are you Hugh McLaren?" the man asked. "Married to Sarah McLaren?"

Hugh paused, searched the man's expression, looked at the road behind him, at the squad car idling in the road, its domed red light on the roof, then back to the man. "Yes, I am," Hugh said.

"Mr. McLaren," the man said, "I'm sorry, but there's been an accident."

CHAPTER TWO

There was no need for an alarm. He'd always had more trouble staying asleep than waking up. It wasn't just his age—the deep creases on thinning skin, the creaking bones, the stiff, popping joints, getting winded from nothing. It was the pain of the voids that surrounded him, the conspicuous silence. He lay under the rise and fall of his faded quilt, staring up at the cedar paneling in the glow of the streetlamp filtering through a thin gray curtain.

The whoosh of the wind rose and fell but never fully subsided. At times, he heard the frantic dance of pine boughs bending to the gusts of bitter cold, the whistle of gaps in the walls. Dry snow pattered like grains of sand on the glass of the old windowpanes. He breathed deeply, though it pained him. So much worse than just a month ago. The weight on his chest had been growing, but in the past month, it had gotten sharp, and he could feel the catch coming. Worse, each time it came, he was reminded of the clock that was ticking on his future, reminded of the sickness, the darker meaning of this rattle. But he managed to stop the cough before it started, delayed the rib-splitting agony and the red soaked rags at least for now, closing his eyes in concentration.

He focused on the howling wind outside, thinking of the snow and the lake. He imagined snow blowing from his roof down to the great shore of Lake Superior and sweeping across the smooth ice pack, rushing across that open expanse before colliding with columns of steam rising at the water's edge. He knew it well, how that comparatively warm water turned to cloud under the onslaught of such frigid temps, visible across miles of open expanse. On a calm morning, it stood like a wall against the rising sun. On a morning like this one, it would be veiled by the storm.

More importantly, he knew the storm raised fish from the deep. Huge beasts accustomed to cold water would move up, following thermoclines until they were within reach of holes augered in the growing pack.

That led Hugh to finally push back the covers and creak out of bed: the thought of those beasts from the deep. Of dropping a jewel of a lure, the tantalizing twist of bait into the unknown darkness below.

Down in the kitchen, he made thin coffee, toasting two slices of bread while the coffee maker churned. He pulled the crusty slices from the toaster and put two new ones in, then set the first on a plate and spread thick layers of peanut butter. When the toaster clicked again, he repeated the process with jam. He pressed the slices together for two sandwiches. The first, he placed in a small paper bag, twisting it shut at the top. That one was for the ice. The second one was breakfast.

Crunching bites and sipping coffee, he looked out the small window above the sink. The wind still howled, spinning snow into drifts. There was no light other than the muted glow of streetlights and porch lamps shining small pools in the haze of the whiteout blizzard. He couldn't see beyond the first two houses. He expected the weather would calm as dawn approached, but that was still hours away.

From the refrigerator he pulled a slab of raw sliced bacon, two eggs, and uncooked hash browns wrapped in butcher paper. He set these on a towel spread across the counter and then cracked the eggs into a small jar and firmly twisted the cap. *That should be enough for the day*, he thought. Gathering the corners of the towel, he wrapped the ingredients tightly into a bundle and imagined the sounds of spattering grease and blowing wind on the ice. It filled him with calm.

He picked up the carafe of coffee and swirled it. *Should be plenty.* He poured it through the narrow top of a battered steel thermos and turned the lid tight.

Thermos and bundle in hand, he left the kitchen, setting them down on the wood floor between the living room and his little attached garage, accessed through a small doorway and a narrow set of unlit stairs. Using the walls for balance, he stepped down. The handle on the door was rimed with frost, and the metal burned his hand. He instinctively reached for the unseen coat hook and donned his stiff work jacket. It was just as frozen as the handle, but other than tucking his hands into the lined pockets, he didn't react to the sudden cold. Still in the dark, he felt the string and clicked on the light.

It had been weeks since he'd last been on the ice, but his equipment sat ready to go, tucked neatly into the old military surplus sledge. So many of the other fishermen had the latest gear, folded neatly on svelte black sleds that popped up to form shelters. But Hugh had grown up fishing with his father, one of the stubborn old-timers, feeling the cold of early predawn mornings marching out across the creaking pack on Lake Superior. He'd always pulled his own sledge, carried his own weight, fought his own battles over hummocks and pressure ridges. Though the two of them had fished together, his father had managed to make it a solitary experience. It hadn't bonded them as much as provided a shared, silent suffering. He'd learned how to keep to himself and to be alone. He swore he'd never be like his father. He remembered the old man's gruff response when asked how he was doing: "Well, I'm here, aren't I?" As if existing were enough. It wasn't. It hadn't been enough for him to have a father who was present but unreachable. It hadn't been enough for his father either. That lonely existence had helped to push away friends and family for years.

Now an old-timer himself, Hugh still preferred fishing in the open air, and he still preferred his old trusty sledge. It was a military surplus unit. It had been snow white but had aged to gray. And yet, the lashing still held, the cover was intact, and the skids still crunched over snow and ice. He'd never had the poles or the belt to pull it, just a loop of rope in his hand or over his shoulder.

He slid the kit from the shelf and lowered it to the ground. Painfully, he knelt down and, with his arthritic, swollen hands, untied the cover and peeled it back to explore the contents of the pulk. The old canvas crinkled in protest. Inside was a mélange of fishing equipment, its vintage spanning the past one hundred years: twists of wire, flags, metal scoops and pliers. There was also a depth meter wrapped in cable, surplus camp foam pads of various sizes, a heavy metal flashlight, a coal shovel, a hatchet, a green canvas camp chair, and his hand auger, itself a relic from old times. He shifted the pieces around and found the rest: the cast-iron skillet, a folded canvas tarp, and mixed hemp and nylon cordage.

He was missing a blanket. Standing up, he found the shelf of gear and pulled down a bulging sack, his surplus sleeping bag inside. This would fill one-third of the sledge, but on a day like today, it would more than earn its space. He removed the depth meter and a few of the other items, then shifted the rest around to make room. He stuffed the sleeping bag deep into the back of the sled where its comparatively light weight might help balance the load. He stood slowly and appraised the sledge. He moved the pieces in his mind, peeled them back to reveal what was underneath. The pulk was ready to charge out into the storm, but he was still missing the most important part.

His tackle was kept inside the house, safe from the drifting snow and the mice. He tucked the canvas shut and rose stiffly to go back to the house. Stooping through the door, he creaked down the narrow steps, his bony hand sliding along the thick paint of the bluestone foundation wall. He pulled the string of the bare bulb and harsh light pooled around him. His workbench was there, with his pack and his tackle.

He pulled out two fishing rods. Their short length and miniature reels made them seem like children's toys, but they were the classic style for ice fishing because there was no need to cast. Drop a line, feel, and wait. There'd certainly be plenty of the latter. He ran a thumb along the line where it came off the spool. It was a taut strand, working its way from reel to eyelet, down through the series of ceramic-lined circles to the minuscule one at the end of the rod before bending back again and retracing its steps outside the eyelets. At the end of the line was a small brass snap swivel, its eye clipped around the base of the first eyelet. The monofilament felt strong, true, and yet so delicate that it was hard to imagine the fight it would need to withstand. This thin string could snare those monsters of the deep, pluck a master of its world from the water, and drag it into the universe of the above. It was the closest thing to magic that he'd seen. He inspected the other rod, and finding it similarly appointed, set the pair aside. Still, he pulled a fresh spool of line off the wall and placed it with the rods. *Can't be too careful*, he thought.

Beneath the workbench, he pushed aside boxes, bins, and cases until he found what he was looking for. It was a metal case the size of a miner's lunch box. It was battleship gray, the paint textured like sandpaper. The top had a smooth silver handle on a hinge, and the lid was sealed with a metal clasp over a loop for a lock. He ran his fingers over its surface, over dents, scrapes, scratched paint, and corners burnished to raw gleaming metal. Each blemish was a reminder of what it had been through, a past written in long-healed scars. He lifted it and set it next to the rods and line with such care that it barely made a sound.

Standing up, he stroked the stubble on his chin. *Still need bait.*

He crossed the room to an ancient refrigerator just at the edge of the pool of light. He pulled the chromed handle, and a bare bulb lit the interior and several small wire shelves holding a smattering of leftovers and a small stack of plastic tubs. The top tub was heavy in his hand and sloshed with water. The lid was tight, and he worked to peel it back. Inside was a little sea of life as the silver-black shapes of shiners swam lazily in the cold. He reached in and swirled his hand, felt the familiar tap and slip of the small fish against his skin. He pulled his hand and let the water drip back into the tub, then brought the tub over to the sink and pulled a matching container from the cupboard overhead. He filled it with cold water. He strained the water out of the tub with the shiners, and the fish slapped against the sudden emptiness before he dumped them into the fresh water. They tumbled clumsily, then set to slow circles. He replaced their lid, rinsed the old one and put it in the cupboard, then brought the fish back to the fridge and set the tub on the shelf next to the others. In the next tub he found what he was looking for, little slivers of gray fish flesh suspended in water. Cisco meat. He pulled the thin strips from the tub and dropped them one by one into a clean Ziploc bag. He set the bag on the bench next to the other equipment and weighed the small pile in his mind. It would do.

He took the bundle back up the narrow stairs and into the garage. There, he tucked it carefully into the sledge, each parcel finding a snug home. From the garage shelf, he plucked a weathered camp stove. It was a squat thing, like a miniature propane tank topped with a stove burner. It was brown from years of use and rattled and jangled with the slightest touch. He held it to his ear and swirled it. White gas sloshed heavily inside. *Plenty for a morning's worth of bacon*, he thought, *and maybe a midday fish fry.* Into the pulk.

With the sledge ready to go, he retreated to the warmth of the house and slowly ascended the stairs to his bedroom. He went to his closet and found a set of long underwear, woolens, and socks, laying them atop his side of the bed like a scarecrow. Sitting at the edge of the bed, he carefully changed from his nightclothes and donned the layers, one after the other.

The bed was flanked on either side by a small nightstand. His side was a tangle of faded quilt and sheets. This, he pressed flat, evened out the comforter, and pulled the fabrics to the corners. The other side was already crisply made, sheets tucked, quilt smoothed. Still, he went to the edges all the same, pushed the hospital fold at the corner, pulled the comforter taut, and ran his calloused hands over the bedding to smooth out imagined creases. He did this automatically, but with reverence. It was his ritual, his practice. Every morning, returning to this side of the bed to set it just so. Every morning unchanged.

When they met, Sarah had taken a chance on him. She'd gotten pregnant, so they made it official in order to appease her family and placate his father, and because it seemed like it was their duty, given the circumstances. Despite the rush of their marriage, they were happy together. Mr. and Mrs. Sarah and Hugh McLaren. Sarah had been a buoy for his lost soul, bringing him into the world of the known, a fixed point upon which he could rely and relate. He felt different with her: found and seen. Their little family thrived in the flowing culture of the seasons of Duluth, Minnesota—watched sunrises from their upstairs windows and threw rocks at Brighton Beach. They watched the ships pass through the canal and covered their daughter's ears against the blasting salute of the horn and the dissonance of the bridge's response. They felt the silence of the place as snow and ice enveloped the world. He felt new and alive.

Not much more than a year after their second child came, Sarah was gone. And with her, his world. He felt himself slide. He couldn't do it. He looked into the small scrunched-up face of that crying baby and realized he would never be the father his son deserved. Still, it took him years to admit it—years of being there but emotionally unavailable, a stoic shadow that could never connect. He lingered, as if waiting for the ghost of their mother to step in and help lift him back up into being a good parent.

It was worse when his daughter was old enough to notice he'd changed. That he wasn't the father she'd once known. It pained him to think of it, her big, curious eyes and her innocent, mirthless tone. "Why are you so quiet?" She didn't even call him Dad anymore. Just "you." They'd been at dinner, her younger brother in a booster seat and her with her shoulders just peeking above the dinner table. Their mother's space sat empty at the head of the table, as it always was since she died. Hugh had been across the room under a pool of light in front of the corner lamp, away from the table in his sitting chair, silently turning the big pages on that morning's *News Tribune*. He folded the paper shut and looked across the room at those big eyes. They bored into him in a way he'd not felt since he was a boy—he knew it was the same look he'd given to his father the day after his mother had left, after the missed meals and the yelling and the bruises. Hugh had come into this same room to find his father a shadow in the same chair.

"What do we do now?" Hugh asked.

After a long blank stare, Hugh's own father turned away. After an even longer pause, he uncorked the whiskey from the side table and poured three fingers of amber into the thirsty glass. Then he just sat there, sliding the tumbler back and forth as if it were swaying at the table of a ship's galley. Hugh looked on, his lip turning down farther and farther while his eyes filled with tears that never fell. Eventually, his father stood, lifted the glass and the bottle from the table and left the room, still looking away. Hugh shut his eyes tight, and his tears dropped to the carpet as he silently wept.

His eyes pressed shut, Hugh willed away the memories, pushed his father away, the pain of losing Sarah, the sting of his daughter's words. What did any of it matter now anyway? He'd lived with the pain of that loss for so long. It had eaten at him until he gave up all he had left and pushed his children away. He'd felt that hole in his core for decades, knowing it was wrong and that if he dug deep enough, he might find the little bit left of himself and could be there for them again. They might accept him and he could be their father again; they might love him and he them. But he couldn't find that part of himself. That part had died with Sarah. He'd fought with those decades of regret. Now, though, it all seemed so inconsequential, all that time spent worrying about what he'd done and what he hadn't, and suddenly he had none left. He thought of those words that were now a part of his vocabulary, words that can change everything: *metastatic sarcoma*.

He had been in the doctor's office for a rough bout of pneumonia that he just couldn't kick. Hugh had fought with it for weeks, and it had settled hard in a wet cough that would leave him bundled over, a sleeve or kerchief spittled with red. He wheezed through a chest X-ray and was sitting in the thin-walled exam room, trying not to listen to the conversation going on in the next room. The doctor was talking loudly, the other person's voice only a dark murmur so that it was a nearly one-sided conversation. Hugh tried to ignore it and wait for his own, wondering who might listen to his consultation through those thin walls. But when his doctor finally came in, his voice was different. He was quiet. He asked Hugh's name and birthdate in words that were breathy and closed, like he was about to start a yawn that never came. The man held his chin forward, eyes down at a piece of paper.

"Mr. McLaren, I'm Dr. Wokski," the doctor said, offering a quick, weak handshake as he stepped softly over to a short leather stool in front of the computer. He pulled a badge from a string to a reader, and the computer beeped to life. "We got your chest X-ray back, and it looks like you do have pneumonia." He searched the screen with his head tilted back as if looking through bifocals, though he wore no glasses. He eventually found the right chart and made a series of clicks before turning the screen toward Hugh. Images appeared dark, with two lobes and a frame of ribs bright against the shadow.

The doctor took a pen from his pocket, clicked it open, and pointed it at the screen. "These are your lungs here and here. You can see this cloud is kind of lighter down there, and that's the fluid in your lungs," he said, drawing loops at the bottoms of the lobes. Then he found a constellation of brightness, like the climbing head of a thunderstorm a quarter of the way up one of the lobes. Within the clouds were pale inky drops. "But the imaging also found a mass, Mr. McLaren. Well, really, a number of them. And that's much more concerning. That's certainly part of why you're having such, um, trouble with your breathing, but, it's, uh, something we need to learn more about, something we need to get figured out," he said. "And soon."

Hugh watched with detachment. As Dr. Wokski sat waiting for a reaction, Hugh searched his mind for what to say. He felt heat at his neck and a dryness in his throat that hadn't been there minutes before. He was just sick. He just had this damned cold. Now he was being told something else was wrong? No, it was just this damned cold.

Then he remembered how it had started for his father. That damned cold. He'd sputtered and sworn at it, too, until a doctor had told him it was something else.

Hugh suffered through a whirlwind of sudden tests and scans, CTs and biopsies, and on Monday he'd be in another office, a mirror of the first, with a different doctor to learn what might be done and how little time he had.

But by now, he already knew it was terminal.

The same thing had killed his insufferable father, cancer that had spread to his lungs and spleen. It had been aggressive for him. Six months. The diagnosis had spelled a kind of freedom for Hugh then. But now it meant he was running out of time.

Hugh found himself leaning on the edge of the bed, still in no more than his long johns. The wind gusted again, brought him back to the moment. It reminded him: These layers keep you alive in cold like this.

Thoroughly bundled from long underwear to wool overshirt and pants, he returned to the kitchen. He picked up his phone from its place on the counter and turned it in his hand. The screen lit with the motion, and he looked at its blankness. No calls. He shouldn't have been surprised. Still, he couldn't deny the hope for a call or a text from his daughter. He'd hoped that maybe Lauren would have listened to his message, that it would have convinced her to put aside the pain of decades and call him back. But he'd burned that bridge a long time ago, and the blank screen was just one more part of his penance. He took a deep breath, his mouth a thin line of disappointment, and let the air puff out through his nose. He pushed the button on the side of the phone, and the screen went dark. He set it back on the counter.

Turning, he went to the closet near the garage and found his old parka. It had once been white but was worn gray from years in spindrift and minding sooty fires. It was large, bulky, just right for Minnesota winters. Around the hood was a rim of coyote fur for the wind. He slid each arm into the enormous sleeves and flattened the hood back over his shoulders. Next, he pulled on his tanned moose-hide mukluks, smoothing the weathered gray canvas uppers below his knees. He donned thin wool gloves, stuffing enormous leather mitts into the parka's pockets. Last, he stretched a black wool watch cap over his head and wrapped a scarf around his neck.

He was ready to go.

He retrieved the small pile of things he'd prepared, turned out the lights, and went to the garage. In his layers, the cold felt more comfortable than in the house. He placed the last of his equipment in the pulk, then dutifully tucked the canvas to protect what was inside. He then threaded the last bit of cord through eyelets and straps and cinched the bundle tight. The result was a snug pack, a rather streamlined-looking sledge. He took the lead line from the end and turned the sledge toward the door, the quiet space suddenly alive with the grind of sand against concrete and fiberglass and metal. He pulled back the lock and lifted the garage door.

The howl of wind and snow was a wall of noise after the quiet. Snow whipped through the opening. He pulled the pulk out into the white, then ducked back into the garage to turn out the light. In the darkness, he ran through a list in his head. *One last thing.* He found the hook between the studs at the edge of the door and lifted his ice picks: two six-inch dowels strung together with parachute cord, nails poking out the end of each. They'd help him get back onto the ice if he fell through. These went into the outside pocket of his parka.

That's everything. He pulled the garage door by a dangle of rope, slowing it down to rest on the ground. He normally locked this door, but never when he went out to fish. The thought of relying on a key to get back into his house if he was cold and wet gnawed at him.

The blizzard howled and blew, but the blanket of storm was calming to him. He'd be alone. He usually was. But with this weather, there would be no one on the roads and no one else out on the ice. There were no external pressures, no burdens of greetings and conversation. All of Duluth was in hibernation. Asleep. That suited him just fine. He was free. Free to his thoughts, and his own timeline.

Surrounded by houses, by city, by people sleeping warm in their beds, he was now even more perfectly alone than he'd been in his own house. The sun was still hours from rising. There was just the glow from a few porch lights and streetlamps, fuzzy from the snow, like the dim torch of a lightning bug. Buildings were dark forms, the spaces between, gray voids. Still, the white of the snow reflected those pools of light, filling even the darkest shadows with the slightest hint of space. Even far from the weak reach of streetlights, Hugh would be able to walk easily without the help of a lamp. That calmed him, too—the anonymity of walking in the dark without a light. A light is a beacon. It's for lighting your way, of course, but it shines for others too. It's a signal that you're there, a person attached to that star. Without it, you can be a ghost in the shadows. It filled him with a fire of excitement that warmed him more than the many layers.

With that, he stooped down and picked up the line of the sledge. Wrapping his hand around it, he turned away from his home and toward the alley, toward the road, and down to the lake. Soon, even his footprints would be filled or scoured by drifting snow and wind. There would be nothing to mark his passing.

CHAPTER THREE

Hugh towed his sledge down the cushion of snow in the center of the street. Fourteenth Avenue was a field of untouched white, awash with windswept banks and berms and valleys. The plows seemed to be waiting for the storm to end. He scoffed at the thought of waiting to do your job until the worst was over. Waiting would just make it harder for everyone. And yet, on this morning, he appreciated the untouched streets. No cars could pass through until the plows came.

Fourteenth was steep. Others were still steeper, where the sledge would have bitten at his heels and taken off down the hill to the lake. On those streets, he would have been better off climbing aboard the sled and holding on. But on this more modest slope, with its thick cushion of snow, the sledge kept right where he wanted it, following faithfully just at the end of its leash.

It was nearly a straight shot down to the water, and were it not for the storm, he would be able to see the lake. London Road was another snowfield. He'd seen this view his entire life. He knew it well, summer and winter. On a clear day, he'd be able to see miles of Lake Superior's flat water or ice and, beyond that, the gentle hills of Wisconsin. But this morning, it was a pale-yellow wash of snow under sodium-vapor streetlamps.

He imagined the view in early summer. The Rose Garden, just across the street, would be filled with flowering bushes, a blanket of green grass, big leafy trees, and row upon row of carefully pruned rosebushes. And in June, all those people running on London Road for the marathon, crowds lining the street, handing out food and encouragement. There would be police cars and sponsors, water cups and balloons, and noise. All that noise. He thought of the sheer activity of it, of how different a place it would be. The curb would be covered in onlookers standing or in lawn chairs. Staring at what? At people plodding along, exhausted. All that wasted energy made no sense to him.

Snow or not, he wondered how many more times he might get to see this street. He thought again of those damned cells dividing and conquering their way through his body, how they were at that very instant multiplying and taking with them the very air he was breathing. He shook his head at the thought. Here at least, he didn't have to worry about disappointing anyone. Out in the cold was the only time he felt that kind of peace. So he shifted in his mukluks, tucked his face deeper into the scarf, and tightened his hood.

He pulled the sledge over the invisible curb onto the promenade of the Rose Garden and angled past the gaudy cupola toward a footbridge at the other end of the park. To his left was a fence guarding a twenty-foot cliff above an old railroad grade. Beyond that was the paved section of the Lakewalk, then trees, then an even taller cliff that dropped to Lake Superior itself.

The wind whipping from the hill found an eddy and calmed some. He could feel the lake, close now.

Trudging on, he reached the bridge, crossed it, and followed the zigzag of ramps down to the path below. He turned right, away from the grandstand of Leif Erikson Park, and headed northeast along the

Lakewalk. More virgin snowdrifts, the sledge rising and falling over the crests like waves.

After a quarter mile, he reached a grove of poplars and birch. He turned off the trail and descended between the trees, the wind a whistling chorus in their boughs.

Out from the trees, the wind returned to a dull, ebbing whoosh as it carved snowdrifts in the open. Troughs in the snow revealed swaths of stone and the smooth undulations of a peninsula of bedrock that sloped down to the water and the lake beyond. Hugh stepped carefully, feeling along with his mukluks in the muted light. The sledge bumped along behind him, lurching and dragging with the changing angles until finally finding the calm, flat surface of the ice.

The lake.

He paused on the ice, taking a moment to drape his picks across his shoulders and absorb the place. From here it would be easy, he thought, flat and straightforward. The glow of streetlights was all behind him, though they were all but invisible in the snow. Ahead was the open dark of ice and then frigid water. And because of the storm, it was all his. There would be no tracks to break him from his focus as he trudged out, no other encampments he'd need to work around. It was just him and the weather, him and the ice and the fish.

Stepping forward again, he folded his hands together behind his back, felt the tug of the line of the sledge as it caught and began to slide along once more. The ice had enough snow to give him traction, but there were spots where the surface was polished like glass. His mukluks handled both the ice and the snow well, and transitioning between them was easy. Besides, his pace was slow enough that he wouldn't slip regardless of his footwear. People slip when they're in a hurry. If you go at the pace of the ice, you'll never slip. The skids of the sledge alternated between a glassy grind of ice and the sandpaper whoosh of snow as he went.

He plodded on until he lost track of how far he'd gone, and then stopped. Out here, the wind was fiercer. As quiet as it had been on shore, it was even quieter on the ice, as if the whole space was absorbing sound so that he could feel how vast it all was. The wind sounded hollow around him, the whistle of it in his parka and the sledge and the lines louder than in the miles of ice around him.

Looking back toward shore he could barely make out anything of the city. There was a gray halo in that direction from the diffused streetlamps and buildings. He visualized the ice pack he'd seen the day before, the distance he'd come, and figured he was about two-thirds of the way to the edge, maybe a shade over a mile. He wouldn't drill at the pack's edge. That was foolhardy, risky. But he did want to see the edge, to get an idea of how it looked, estimate the quality of the ice. So he kept on.

At the inky black of the edge of the pack where the ice stopped, a tiny drop-off marked the boundary between solid ground and the open waters of Lake Superior. Just behind it, where Hugh stood, the ice underfoot looked and felt firm, same as he'd found since leaving shore. Things looked good, solid. It wouldn't be many more days before the pack grew to cover much of this end of the lake. It was not uncommon to be able to walk from Minnesota to Wisconsin come January, although it had been a few years since the last decent ice-over. With a few more of these cold nights, though, and calmer wind, this year's ice might even cover the whole lake.

He thought of Isle Royale up north on the lake. In the coldest winters, when the ice froze solid and made a bridge from the mainland to the island, wolves would traverse from one to the other. It had been a long time since they'd made that crossing, which meant a world of hurt to the animals on both ends. Trapped on the island, the few wolves remaining were dying out from their inbred stock, while the moose were growing sickly and crowded, lacking the natural culling of the herd that the wolves helped to accelerate. The sick and weak were left to live and drain the resources of the growing population. He imagined that lonely journey of a wolf across that expanse of ice. What would draw an animal across such desolation, over such distance? *Ha*, he thought, *what drives me to do it?* He was different from a wolf, though. He had intention. That's what made him different. The wolf had needs and instinct but not intention. Or did it?

He refocused. It was still early in the season, but the ice he found showed good progress. This was good ice, and he felt safe on it.

Safe, he thought. The word pulled at a long-distant memory. It turned for a moment in his mind like fog tumbling in curls, images manifesting from the gray murk. He was back at the house in Duluth. Afternoon light arced through western windows, glittering in golden shafts. There were the kids. Jason, still just a baby, lay on his back on a blanket, staring up at the shine and a dangle of colored shapes just within reach. Lauren stood at the couch in front of a collection of books, her tummy against the cushions as she turned colorful pages of shapes. They were quiet together.

Their mother stepped silently into the room, her dish apron still on. She looked at the children, then at him. They shared a quiet smile, and she stepped toward him, his arm finding its place around her waist. They looked on at the love before them. He lifted his hand and felt the smooth warmth of the skin of her arm and pulled her close. He wished he had turned her toward him, to tell her what was coming. But as their heads touched, the vision was broken, and he was back in the dark cold.

He thought of that moment. He thought of it often. She'd helped him become the loving father and husband he wanted to be, and they made it, made a family. There it was cast in golden light, their idea of perfection with moments of laughter, the incredible mayhem of two kids, and those moments of wonder when he could step back and see the four of them all together.

He'd been a fool not to tell her. He could have told her how much she meant to him. He could have. He should have. But the words hadn't come, so he'd tried to show it. That's more important, isn't it? To show your love? But there's no closure there. You have to say it. He'd meant to. But he'd missed his chance and never said it. He thought of what he'd say now. *You're a good mother, so good to our little boy and girl, and they love you. And I love you. Don't ever forget that.* It was easier to think of what to say about the kids than himself. He hadn't known where to start with himself, other than he didn't know what he'd do without her. But he knew the answer to that now.

His eyes were welling, and the cold wind threatened to freeze the tears before they even fell. He blinked and touched his mitten to the spot to blot them away. He looked at the dark chop of water, at that stark line where the pack ended and the cold endlessness began.

Taking a deep breath, he turned away from the edge and retraced a hundred paces. This would be the place.

CHAPTER FOUR

Hugh dropped the tow rope. Kneeling next to the sledge, he pulled at the loose ends of the drawcord that secured the sledge contents. The loops on the bows shrank, then disappeared, and the knots popped. He opened the cover and reached inside. He pawed at the contents in the dark until he found the old coal shovel. It was big and heavy, a square metal blade, all rusted with corners bent. The shaft was thicker than a spade but much shorter. He rose, using the shovel for leverage on the way up. Resting the blade on the ice, he scraped it across in strips, walking slowly, no sharp movements. He was in no hurry. So many kids shoveled like it was a race, go go go, flip, toss, throw, huff and puff. He'd be breathing hard, no doubt, but he'd take his time.

He stopped to catch his breath often, resting on the shovel and taking in the thrum of storm around him. It seemed to be calming some. The peaks of the gusts were less intense, and the driving snow had slowed. That would be good for his exposed position on the ice. It would make each of his tasks easier.

He was making headway against the snow, and a rectangle of clear ice was forming. It was dark blue and pale white. Where it was white, it looked like most other winter lakes, an opaque shield. Where it was dark, it looked like volcanic glass, deep blues and bending light. It formed like a sort of magic in his mind. This ice was hard ice, and it made him feel good, confident that it would hold true. It rang against the shovel, and after a time, the bit of the drill would bite into it as if boring through stone—clean cuts, hard earned.

With the space clear, he returned the shovel to the sledge and felt for the auger. It was a bulky thing that dictated the arrangement of everything around it: an old manual model, with polished wooden handles on the offset shaft that rose from the bit. The blade itself was over three feet long and painted blue. It turned in four huge curls like a playground's slide. At its tip were two heavy blades of carbon steel bolted to the twisting shaft. He kept this part oiled to keep the metal from rusting, and they shone even in the darkness.

He hauled the awkward thing over to the dark patch of shadow ice. With care, he lifted the auger vertical and rested the tip of the bit on the ice. He paused there, waiting. He looked around. With the wind just barely calmer, he could see more of the pack, though it was still dark. Beyond was the faint glow of the city. It was far enough away that, even without the wind, he doubted a shout would reach someone standing on the shore. That suited him. People had always been the biggest source of problems in his life. The biggest source of pain, of regret. He thought of his children. They were grown now and living their own lives. He'd separated himself from them when their mother had died. He hadn't gone anywhere, hadn't sent them away, but he'd become distant. He did the bare minimum: changed them, dressed them, got them to school and appointments on time, and shushed them in the supermarket. He didn't know what to do when they cried, how to console them for their loss. He felt it too, but held himself back. It was unfair to him. This was unfair. To have these two vulnerable kids, and to have so little love to give. He tried, but everyone was relieved when it came time for each of them to go off to school, to leave home and strike out on their own lives. That was his love, to hold on just long enough. His love was to make sure they made it to the point where they could take over. It was all he could do. It took everything. It was a singular focus, a specific goal, and yet it filled him with regret. They'd gone. He'd pushed them away. And now, he felt the void of that loss, the void of those voices gone from his house, and the opportunities he'd missed. He should have done better, done more. But hadn't he given all that he could?

Hugh thought of his own childhood, of his mother. It was so long ago, and he'd been so young.

He was tucked away, peeking through the slats of the hall closet door. He knew he wasn't supposed to be there. He'd been told to go to bed, to stay in his room. And he knew that meant his parents were fighting.

His mother was standing at the kitchen sink, working at a pile of dishes, the dim light casting her back in blue shadow. Her movements were tight and quick. She had started with her eyes down at the sink, but now her gaze was fixed out the window, past the reflection of her stare. She was somewhere else. Perhaps she was replaying a conversation. Or the day. Or coming home to a mess of a house and a husband who had hardly gotten off the couch the entire day. She was stoic, staring, silent.

His father stood at the back of the kitchen, hands in pockets. His breath shallow, waiting.

After a long while of silent scrubbing, without moving her gaze from its fixed point out the window, she spoke. "I'm leaving tonight," she said.

His mouth pressed into a thin line, and his elbows tightened against his sides as if a cold breeze had just blown in.

"I won't be coming back."

His father stood there, dumb and silent, his face blank until he took a breath to speak.

"I . . ." he said. He lingered on the word, but she interrupted him.

"It doesn't matter," she said, now turning toward him, crossing her arms, still dripping, across her chest. "You're going to stay here and do whatever the hell you want, but I'm done." She turned back to the sink, pulling a towel from the rod and wiping her hands and arms dry. Her voice rose and her cheeks flushed. "I'm not going to push you anymore, I'm not going to listen to you complain anymore. I'm exhausted. I'm tired of it, and I'm tired of being around it."

She tugged the towel back onto the rack and untied her apron.

"You're going to have to figure it out," she said. "Because you're on your own."

She threw the ball of apron at his chest, and it slumped at his feet. He hadn't moved. His hands were still in his pockets, and his eyes clouded. She left the room, and he stayed there, stock-still while the sounds of doors, drawers, and zippers drifted through the house. Soon, bags were packed next to the door, and then they were gone. Hugh heard the car start, click into drive, and then motor away. And then the house was silent. His father just stood there in the kitchen, hands still in his pockets.

Hugh blinked away the thought, felt the weight of the auger again as it leaned on him. He looked down at the tip, at the delicate, razor-sharp angles of steel. The metal was bare, the sharpened edges clean, shining in the dim light like a keen blade. He shifted the auger until it was standing straight up. He flexed his hands, felt the polished wood handles through his mitts, their easy spin over the metal core. Turning the handles carefully, the tip bit into the ice, crystals pooling around it.

Slowly at first to keep the bit from skipping, he worked the metal until the hole was deep enough that he felt confident it would stay true as he drilled. Then, he stood upright and sped up. Shaved ice came from the hole in curls, some of it joining the blowing snow. The whoosh and scrape of the auger melded with the sound of the wind, and he was consumed with the work.

All of the packing and hauling and spindrift were working up to this point. And from here, there'd be the quiet of frozen water.

The auger descended into the ice until it popped free into openness below. When he pulled it back up, water sloshed from the hole, spilling out around it and soaking the shaved ice. He lifted the auger clear and carried it back to the sledge. He was careful not to set it back on the ice, lest it become welded there by the water dripping from it.

Back at the hole, he knelt and looked at it. It was perfectly round, and its edges were smooth. The precision of the drilling had always fascinated him. In the dark he couldn't see the thickness of the ice, so he took off a mitten, removed the wool liner glove underneath, and reached his now bare hand into the hole. His fingers followed the edge of the ice, the surface rifled from the auger's downward progression. The water felt warm, and it was, probably forty degrees warmer than the air around him. The comfort of the water felt like a siren song, a temptation for more agreeable surroundings. *Come in*, it seemed to beckon. *It's so much warmer here.* But it would be short-lived comfort. At just above freezing, it was hardly hospitable. Three minutes in the water and he'd be in bad shape, begin losing his senses, his teeth chattering as his muscles fumbled and his brain fogged. Hypothermia and frostbite. Both of them are nefarious, sneak up silently. You can be completely unaware and end up in a bad way before you know it. You always have to be vigilant, aware of your surroundings, aware of what you're feeling. Aware of what you can't feel anymore.

Finding the bottom of the hole, he stretched his fingers to measure the surface. Four inches by his estimate. He laughed. Exactly what the authorities deemed safe for ice fishing. He couldn't remember the number of times he'd checked and found the ice much thinner. But when the ice is right, it's fine. This ice was right. Glassy, dense, solid.

He removed and unfolded the camp chair, then returned to the sledge for his fishing equipment and bait. The preset snap swivels made adding a jig easy, just a pop of an eyelet and the threading of metal through the lure. He took the tackle box and gingerly placed it on the ice, being sure to keep it a safe distance from the hole. When he opened the clasp and raised the lid, trays levered up and out to reveal a treasure chest filled with gems of all colors and shapes. He'd looked in this box thousands of times, but it never ceased to ignite a small spark of wonder.

The tackle seemed to glow in the scant light. The trays were filled with all kinds of lures. Each one was a proven talisman for pulling fish from their world up to ours. Opening the chest revealed to him their charm, as if these lures were hooking him too. They were a beautiful sight, all manner of fluorescent colors, and more natural hues too, and the glint of steel. There were spin baits and crank baits, and spoons, jigs, and sinkers, crawlers, frogs, and leeches, slippery minnows and fuzzy tails. And there were hooks—sharp, barbed hooks all through. Some were small, while others looked like meat hooks. Some were silver, others black, still others red. There were beads, rattles, swivels, sparklers, and leaders. Some of the lures were carved and painted masterpieces, monuments to the fish and creatures that they modeled. Others were abstracted representations, as if drawn in crayon and cut from paper.

He picked at the contents, never catching a hook in his weathered skin. He tweezed out a bright pink jig with an impossibly huge eye painted on the side. From a nearby compartment, he pinched a flexible rubber worm, pure white. This he slid over the sharp end of the hook, headfirst, tracing the arc of the metal as he punctured it from head to tail. Near the end of the curve, he let the metal poke out again. Sliding the worm home, he lined it up perfectly with the hook. With the worm set, he took the swivel and popped it open, lacing the thin wire through the eyelet on the jig before clipping the snap swivel shut.

Pleased with the lure, he hinged the tiny shelves back into place, shut the lid, closed the clasp, and clipped a small carabiner through the loop to secure it. He set the small chest aside.

Transferring the now-tethered jig to his still-mittened hand, he reached into the sledge and picked up the Ziploc of cisco strips. In the bag they looked like bits of gray lutefisk. He removed a piece and, holding it between two fingers, placed it on the hook, less ceremoniously than with the other, but with practiced precision. He hooked it once, then looped it around tightly and put it through the hook once more.

Satisfied with the lure, he walked his hands down the fishing rod and took hold of the reel. It was tiny in his hand. When he gave the large crank a touch, the front of the reel spun wildly, guiding line back onto the spindle as the lure climbed up to the tip of the rod. Pointing it at the hole in the ice, he opened the bail, levering the front loop of the reel out of the way to release the line. The lure dropped into the water with a plop, its bright white reflecting around the circumference of the hole for a moment before disappearing into the shadow.

The line spooled off the reel for what felt like an eternity, little curls of monofilament jumping through the ceramic eyelets of the rod. These were deep waters, maybe ninety feet or more beneath his boots. This was a good spot, a natural funnel that brought hunter and prey together down below. Off to his right, he knew, the little stream that ran under the interstate just east of the Rose Garden kept a steady flow of new prey feeding the area. A channel led down to the bottom of an underwater ridge that terminated under him at a pointed hill of stone. Across the channel, another plateau of rock also dropped off so that the channel formed a sort of canyon, the three meeting here.

Eventually, the line stopped spooling off the reel, stopped dancing through the rod, and it was still. He clicked the bail back into place and slipped the liner glove from his right hand. He tucked the glove into a pocket and took hold of the rod, pulling the line taut and placing his index finger under the line near the reel so he could hold its tension with that one fingertip. He felt so much through that line. He could feel the whistle of wind, which was distracting, but he could feel the action of the rod, and the whoosh of water on lure as he pulled at it, lifting it off the bottom. He let it back down again, holding tension as it dropped. Like a telephone of cups and string, the communication didn't work if the line was slack, so he controlled the descent, let the weight of the jig guide his arm and wrist down until he felt the resolute thud of lake-bottom stone echo up to his fingertip. He could see it now, a shadow of a murky outline way down under the water, his jig disturbing a puff of silt. There would be rocks around there, and bedrock. He knew, based on the amount of line, that he was on the top of the plateau and not the bottom. No matter. This would work as well as any. Through his touch on the line, he continued to envision the lake bottom. It was a dim space of blues and greens and grays. It was quiet, no sound of wind, hardly any sound of moving water.

With the lure in an acceptable position, he reeled in a couple feet of line, then rigged the pole into the framework of his chair. So long as he was sitting on the chair when a bite came, he'd know it, and the rod and chair would stay in place. If he was away when that happened, hopefully the chair would act as a brace against the hole.

He imagined the deep, the world around his lure, the moving shadows of the lake trout. Lumbering shapes silently watching for their next meal, so camouflaged as to nearly disappear. With white bellies for those below and mottled spots across their backs for those above, perhaps their least camouflaged features are shown last—a defined jaw filled with sharp teeth and drawn forever in a frown. They're beautiful fish, built for killing other creatures in the deep. They have evolved for this. Just as he has evolved to catch them.

CHAPTER FIVE

With his rod wedged in the makeshift brace, Hugh's mind turned to breakfast. The weather had begun to calm some, and the wind had died enough to let him run the stove.

The sledge was next to him, and he rifled through it to find the skillet, the stove, and the food. Pivoting on his chair, he prepared everything dutifully, laying out each item so that it was ready when he needed it. He picked up the stove, his mitts taking on streaks of soot. It was like an enormous hand grenade, short and squat and metal. *It could be a grenade*, he thought, *if all that gas ignited.* But it was made to contain the energy not to spill it out. He held it in his lap and began the slow process of pumping it full of air. This would pressurize the tank and allow the gas to flow into the tubing. The pump was a long metal thing, with a little weep hole in the center of the handle that he had to press in order to form a seal. He first tried this with his mitts on, but the air hissed right through the fabric. With a sigh, he removed his glove from his right hand and began pumping again, his bare skin open to the bitter cold. The stove rattled and squeaked, but pressure built steadily in the tank. He continued for a long time, his hand burning in the cold. He set the stove on the ice and picked the lighter from his fan of gear spread before him. When he unscrewed the control knob on the Coleman, little flecks of white gas sprayed out from the nozzle. He closed the valve and held the lighter near the spattered fuel. Flicking the wheel launched sparks and flame at the gasoline. It ignited immediately, the flash incredibly bright in the deep darkness. He held his hand near the flames, and his skin glowed like a red-orange beacon in the dark. He welcomed the meager warmth, but soon, the flames shrank until all that was left was a single pilot light, a little candle at the heart of the burner. Turning the knob now, he released more gas. Instead of spattering liquid, it came out of the burner's many holes as a vapor. It hissed, then caught the pilot light. Blue dots of flame glowed, traveling in a chain reaction around the perimeter of the burner with a little *fump* as it lit at each vent. The stove lit in a full circle of tiny fires, then sputtered bright yellow, then calmed, repeating the process several more times before settling into a steady purr.

The blue glow shone in the darkness, just enough to catch the tops of snowbanks and the edges of his gear. Atop the burner, he placed the cast-iron skillet. He found the bacon and picked at the slices. They were frozen together, so he set the whole block into the skillet and turned up the heat. The stove whirred. The block of bacon slid as the fat rendered and soon a sizzle came from the pan.

He leaned back in his camp chair. You can't rush the fish, and you don't rush bacon. The block would take some time to thaw, he knew, and the fish had a mind of their own. With his hands tucked away, and his many layers, he was comfortable in the cold and wind, staring at the glow of the stove.

As he sat, the wind shifted. It was a subtle change, but after a whoosh and the passing calm of a few gusts, when it came again it was out of the southwest, a nearly ninety-degree shift. Hugh recognized the shift in some background subconscious. It was similar to the earlier wind, but it no longer carried snow. Just cold. Cold and change. But the howl and nuisance were constant companions.

The slices of bacon were beginning to blossom from the block, and he encouraged them, peeling each one back in turn with an ungloved hand. The smell was coming off the skillet now, that unmistakable scent of meat and food and home. It rose in curls of steam like the smoke off the water at the pack edge. He was reminded of a time back at that little house up the hill. A time that now filled him with regret, of wishing he'd done things differently.

—

It was the day after his daughter's commencement. She'd just graduated from Central High School. They were standing in the kitchen as he skittered bacon around the pan.

"You know," he said, his eyes still on the bacon, "now that you're graduated, it's time to start looking for work and a place to live." It came out before he'd even realized it. It was something his father would have said to him. She'd gotten a scholarship and was going to college, something he'd always thought was a waste of time and money. Or, in her case, just time. His suggestion was a jab at her life plan.

It pained him, but he knew it was what she needed. He knew that pushing her away would give her the freedom to live. It would give her freedom from him. He was a weight, and he would drag her down.

She'd come in with a certain lightness, but even out of the corner of his eye, he could see her begin to wither. Her shoulders drooped and her head sank before she slowly pulled back upright.

Her arms crossed, her eyes fixed on a blank spot on the far wall. "I'll be here through the summer," she said, her voice stiff with the tension of jaw and back. "And then you won't have to worry about me."

He pushed the bacon, flipping the darker pieces. "Well, that's a start," he said. "What are you doing for the summer?"

"What do you mean?" she asked.

"Where are you going to live and what are you going to do?" he asked, his eyes still on the bacon.

She scoffed, and her eyes went wet with shine. "I don't know," she said. "I guess I'll get a job."

"Good," he said. "You can start looking and applying today. If you find one in the next week, you can stay here and pay rent."

"You're kicking me out?" she said, her brows pressed together.

"No," he said, "this is just a bit of reality. You're an adult now, and you ought to be doing at least one adult thing or you're going to be damned soon enough." He looked away from the pan now and turned toward her. "It's bad enough that damned scholarship. You're going to think the whole world gets handed to you. And then you spend the next four years or more just going to more school instead of working. Going to school so you can just graduate and end up working the same goddamn job you would have otherwise. It's not how the world works. You've got to make money, and nobody's just going to coddle you through it all like I've been for the past eighteen years."

"Coddle?" she said.

"That's right," he said, "coddle. You've had all the things taken care of for you by someone else who does the work."

Her face went stony, and all emotion drained from it. Her eyes fixed on a point somewhere between them, and she seemed to be trying hard to hold something back. It wasn't until after a long pause that she spoke again.

"Fine," she said. "And I'll look for a place too."

When she left, it was for good.

He knew that he had done the wrong thing, even if it was for the right reason. She'd never realize that he was protecting her from him. He thought back to that version of himself that summer, and it turned his stomach. He was disgusted with himself, disappointed. He knew he had needed to push her to be on her own. He knew he would hobble her from becoming her best self. At the same time, it played out as if someone else were speaking. Someone who had talked to him that way when he was young. He had never truly gotten away from his father. But by Hugh removing himself from her life, she might have a chance at happiness. He'd lost his, and he'd never been able to come back from it. He didn't want that for her. She'd never forgive him, he knew. How could she? He'd spent most of her childhood as a shadow. And now she would be rid of him. She hadn't left on her own terms, but from here out, she'd live on them, free to live and love and make of herself what she wanted.

But all that had changed, hadn't it? He thought of the cells dividing, even then, inside of him, and that clock ticking in the back of his head. He'd broken that silence with her because it was his last chance to try to make things right again. The flat numbness of holding on to the silence was so much worse than the pain of trying, wasn't it? The one thing he'd needed to do was to tell her, so that's what he'd done.

As he stared, the last of the bacon peeled apart and fell gently in the skillet. The sizzle continued, and he pushed it around in the grease with a wooden spoon. It crackled with the movement, and he felt the warm glow from the iron on his face.

He leaned back again, still holding the wooden spoon. With his free hand, he bent down to check the rod. It was still secure. Touching the line with his fingertip, he felt the same tension he'd felt before—the steady pull of gravity. Holding it there, he strained to read the feel of the line, to imagine its surroundings. But there were no fish. He'd have to keep waiting.

Letting go of the line, he grabbed the pack of butcher paper and peeled back the layers to reveal the shredded hash browns inside: pale, almost white crystals of potato. They crinkled like candlestick ice in his hand. With the wooden spoon, he pushed the bacon to the side, then poured the hash browns into the hot grease. They sizzled, and he stirred them to distribute the fat, pressed them evenly, and then sat back once more.

He thought about his daughter, about the tough love he'd given her. He knew she hadn't appreciated it. He hadn't seen her for years and hadn't talked to her for nearly as many. He was foolish to think that she'd call him back. That thought pained him. He knew he'd done wrong by her, but all he'd ever done was try. And still, he couldn't bear being near her. The pain of what she meant to him was too great. She was such a strong reminder of her mother, of all that was gone. So he had pushed her away, just when she needed him. It was much the same with his son, but he'd been even less forgiving. Jason was giving what he'd gotten. Everyone tolerated each other until they could be rid of the anchor of one another. Of Hugh, really. He was the stone that pulled them all down. So it was better for them to be off living their own lives. Better for them, certainly.

That was part of what had made it so hard to call. It was the first thing he'd thought about when he heard his diagnosis, that he had to call his daughter. But he'd been scared that she wouldn't care. That would only be fair. But he hoped that she might have the empathy of her mother, the capacity for caring and love that had opened his heart in the first place. He didn't deserve that, with either of them. But he hoped that his daughter might give him that chance.

He'd been a fool to think she'd pick up, to think she'd call him back. Those were empty hopes.

Leaning forward, Hugh poked at the hash browns. The top layer had thawed, and they were beginning to lace together. Running the spoon along the pan, he felt the firm resistance of crisped potato. He slid the spoon underneath and lifted the latticework from the skillet. He could tell the bottoms were golden by feel. He lifted them in one big sheet and flipped them back onto the pan. It sizzled, and a puff rose from the potatoes. With a practiced disregard for his own skin, he reached in and deftly picked at a piece of bacon, lifting it and setting it on top of the potatoes. His fingers moved quickly, barely touching an edge. Repeating the process, he moved all the pieces, leaving a large empty space beside the potatoes. Taking the jar from the sledge, he wrapped his hand around the lid but startled with pain across his palm. The metal had taken on the cold and burned him. He found his glove and tried once more. The lid gave way, and he poured the still-liquid unscrambled eggs into the pan, the yolks like drops of sunshine among the whites.

He worked the skillet some more, pushed the hash browns, lifted pieces of bacon, and poked at the eggs. Everything looked to be done. So he reached beneath the warm iron and turned the knob on the stove to shut off the gas. He could have turned it off at the burner, but he wasn't planning to use the stove again and wanted to bleed the lines.

He sat back and watched, waited as the last of the fumes flowed through the tubing before the stove sputtered, flickered, and then went dark and quiet. The pan still sizzled, and he leaned toward it to see if he could catch the smell before the wind stole it. He did. A perfect fisherman's breakfast.

Removing a fork from his gear, he carved out a piece of hash browns and took a bite. They were crispy, chewy, and rich. Slicing the edge of the fork through the egg, he pierced the yolk. Its golden filling spilled out, pooling against the white of the egg and the wall of hash browns. It was hot, soothing, fulfilling. He felt it made him ready for anything, like a balm for whatever came next. He knew it would be his last warm meal for a while. He planned to be out here for some time, for the full day. He knew the fish might not bite but also that the journey was much more arduous in the storm and that getting home might take a good deal longer than the way out. Still, he'd be settling in for much of the day if he could.

As he ate his breakfast, he noted that, while the wind still blew stiffly, there was perhaps less snow coming down. He looked around his little camp and could see just a touch farther than before, to more emptiness around him. Such a stark landscape on the ice. No landmarks meant nothing to measure himself against, nothing to remind him of times he'd done wrong, things he should have handled differently. The flat ice was dark where it had formed into thick glass, and there were arcs of snow on top. It looked otherworldly, like those views of the earth from space where bright white clouds stand out against the blue marble of ocean. It made him feel both big and small in the same moment.

He blinked hard and brought himself back to reality. It was cold but for the breakfast, though the wind was quickly draining its heat. He took big bites now, not wanting to lose the warmth. He made quick work of it, enjoying the egg and chewing the crisped hash browns. He dragged the pieces of bacon through the grease before bringing them to his mouth.

The pan was nearly empty when the fishing rod wedged into the camp chair and bent wildly. He felt it against his leg and in the pull of the chair. With composure, he reached down for the rod, taking hold of it with stiff fists that recognized how much force might be on them once it was free of the chair. He tilted it, lifted it, and slid it forward. No longer restrained, he felt the fish on the rod, heavy at the end of the line. A static weight, then a frantic tug. He pulled back against the fish to set the hook if it hadn't happened already, careful to keep tension the whole time. While the fish tugged, the reel whined as line spooled out. He tightened the drag until that calmed some. He slowly cranked on the reel. Line spooled in, the spool slipped with the drag as the fish pulled. He made steady progress, and round and round the line wrapped the reel. Standing up, he lifted the rod, then lowered it, reeling fast against the relaxed tension on the line, the fish coming up in jerks of several feet. He repeated this process until the water began to slosh in the hole. He knew it was close then, and he bent down, kneeling on the ice, reaching his hand down to the frigid water as he raised the rod in the other. When the nose of the fish poked above the surface, he recognized the unmistakable scowl of a lake trout.

"There you are," he said. He slid his hand along its jaw to the sharp line of gills and slipped his fingers underneath it. His fingers found the familiar divot between the bones under the edge of the jaw, the spot where hard bone was draped by nothing but skin. As if God himself made a handle for man on the trout. The fish gave a firm wriggle in the hole, but he had him, and the wriggle only helped propel him up from the water. Standing, he appreciated the weight of the thing. Out of the water, he strained to hold it with his one arm extended. The trout was three feet long and probably twenty pounds. He walked away from the hole to the other side of the sledge and laid it down on the ice. It flapped and wriggled there. He reached into the sledge and found his axe. Without removing the mask from the blade, he turned it so the flat poll was toward the fish's head. He raised it slightly, then swung it down. The block of steel landed with a muffled crunch on the back of the fish's head and the flailing stopped. He held there, not moving for a long time, one hand on the fish, his other on the axe, his knees on the ice.

In the winter, he remembered, his father would drag the fish from their holes, judiciously pull the hook, and then push them away across the ice. They'd skitter across the smooth surface, flopping with dull thuds and thwacks as they went. Before they'd come to a stop, he'd have his line back in the hole, eyes back toward the dark. Hugh could never turn his attention back to the next fish, though. He'd had to watch as the fish flopped and jumped, trying to breathe. The grotesque gasping of their jaws. Their movements would slow, but the intensity of their effort would increase. Eventually, they would suffocate to death. And only after he knew they would not try to breathe again could he look away, look back to his father as he slowly jigged the rod at the hole.

Summers were worse. When they weren't on the ice, his father had kept them on a stringer, a rusty steel rod shoved up through their gills and out the mouth, with a frayed, braided poly rope trailing behind. The fish would all bundle together on this stringer, stacked together. But they'd live like that for hours or days in the water, suspended in a sort of limbo between life and death, trapped until the torture was over. He knew that was part of it. But what bothered him was what came next.

When it came time to eat, his father would pull the stringer and find the fish he wanted. If it was in the middle of the bunch, he'd slide his fillet knife down the gullet and slice the jaw open so he could pop the fish off the stringer without having to unthread the lot of them. The fish would thrash wildly against the mutilation, but he'd pick it up and wheel it over to the fish-cleaning table. It was an old metal kitchen sink, one of the tin ones that grows a patina over time, mounted to plywood on reclaimed wood legs and standing right along shore. At the back of the table was a slot for the offal. The guts would fall down the bank, where the stuff would pile up just beyond the water. It was a beacon for gulls, and they knew to circle when someone stood at the altar. Without fail, his father would take the fish and fillet it alive. Once the fillets were clean off, the body of the fish went down the chute too. And the fish would tumble down to the feeding field where it lay, muscles all gone so that it could no longer twitch but could move its jaws, so that it lay there gasping for air, its sides gone and its jaw moving asymmetrically from coming off the strainer. It horrified Hugh.

He'd learned not to question it because when he asked his father about the practice, he had turned, eyebrows raised, eyes wide. "It's a goddamn fish." His gaze held on him. "What's wrong with you?" he asked. "Do you feel bad for them?" To this, Hugh clammed up and looked away, his hands in a knot behind him and his foot searching for an answer in the dirt. When he looked back at his father, his eyes hadn't moved. "It's a goddamn fish," he said, "and you gotta be a goddamn man." With that, he handed him the knife and had him take over the filleting. It was a horrible memory: the protestations of the fish, the unblinking eye, the gasping, the clinging to life. He'd kept working through tears, followed his father's cold instructions.

He couldn't stand to see them like that. And he never got over it.

So when it came time for him to do it on his own, he always put them out of their misery as soon as he could. He knelt on the ice over his freshly killed fish, hands on his legs. He considered processing the fish right then and putting it in the pan, but he wasn't going to need to eat for a while. So he left it where it lay. That's one of the convenient things with ice fishing: You don't have to worry about keeping the fish fresh. You just leave it out to freeze.

The wind was still as strong as ever, but the light was finally coming.

It was just a faint glow on the horizon now, a brightening of the gray of the storm, but he was beginning to see the shadows of things.

It was one of those mornings where the weather could go in any direction. In a moment, it could disintegrate again to whiteout, or it could clear up and the sun might just put on a show for sunrise. The wind could blow clear through it all or die down. Or maybe it would be off and on for the entire day. You just never knew on the lake.

But for now, the wind and the snow kept on.

He picked up the fish. It was as cold as the water, but not yet as cold as the air and the ice around him. It was limp, and he could feel the mass of muscle on either side. He draped it across his palms like an offering and bowed his head.

"Thank you, fish," he said.

His words were a whisper, and he could barely hear the rumble of his voice in the wind. He set it on the ice to freeze and turned back to the last remaining bites from the skillet. The fat had already hardened in white pools in the pan. *I'll keep that for the fish*, he thought, visualizing the shine of fresh fillets and the sizzle of meat in the tallow.

Setting the pan aside, he turned back to the task at hand and placed another piece of cisco on the hook before dropping it into the hole with a plop. He again placed the rod into the framework of the chair and sat back as if to admire his work. It was all set, and there was nothing to do now but wait.

CHAPTER SIX

He watched the line. The rod was held fast in the chair. He considered jigging it and looked over at the now-frozen trout he'd caught. He hadn't been jigging for that one, he remembered, so he sat back in his chair to listen and watch. He heard the steady rush of all that wind. It wasn't really gusting anymore, more of a steady, unrelenting blow. It always seemed that a blow like that couldn't last, or at least that the snow would move out even if the wind stayed. One of them always peeled off when it got so bad. Like how a summer night so hot and humid that everything stops is always followed by an immense storm, one that breaks the weather and the heat spell, an enormous hammer shattering the peace with sparks and thunder. This wind felt like that to him. It felt like, before long, he'd see the sky open.

He heard the moan of the ice pack protesting against the movement of water. It was like the keen of a whale, from its deep, somber tones to higher-pitched cries. It was normal to hear the ice, but he always paid attention. A scream, a springy crack, the thud of shifting, all that could quickly become important.

He remembered when that couple disappeared just after the New Year up north. They'd taken their snow machines from the cabin and launched out onto the ice of Black Steel Lake. There were candles still burning in the cabin, snacks laid out, but no one home. Just two sets of snow machine tracks leading out onto the lake.

Crews arrived from the sheriff's office and followed the tracks out to the lake, where they were lost in the mess from who knows how many other snow machines. Following all the branches of tracks, they finally found a pair that went all the way to where the Kawishiwi and Black Steel meet. They found open water. Where there's current, the ice doesn't get as thick. The water constantly churns and keeps the ice from forming, and sometimes you'll find fully open water in the cold dead of winter, just from that convection of moving current. It looked like puddles on the ice, big round dark spots in all that white. But they weren't puddles. And the ice got thinner and thinner, so that you couldn't even walk up to the edge without going in. There were a couple of them, these holes, just up from the river. It was cold as heck that week. Who'd have thought that ice would have been open?

There were two sets of tracks that went into those places and never came out. And there was a helmet. They spent days looking for them from there, mostly searching underwater. *My god, you just can't trust the ice.* He knew that more than anyone, and it made him feel hollow. Maybe that couple had known too; they'd just forgotten. In either case, their night had gone from candles, wine, and food in the cabin to a moonlight ride, to gone.

He sat and listened to the pinging of the ice. A newbie on the pack would jump and run at the first sign of it, but the twangs were familiar to Hugh. Over years of being out on hard water, he'd learned to accept them, even be comfortable with them.

But then, as he listened, a ping turned to a thwack, and all thoughts of weather and fish left him.

He sat motionless. He was an animal now, alert to the environment around him, checking for dangers. Then there was a calving sound, a deep rumble punctuated with the staccato of cracks, as if a tree had been felled. He felt the surface under his feet shudder and still. He instinctively grabbed the arms of his chair and checked the ice around him. Seeing no cracks, he checked that his picks still draped over his shoulders and got up. The area around his hole was intact, but he needed to look around further.

Heading toward the face that fronted the lake, he found it unchanged. But the waves on the water were much larger than they had been earlier, a slapping chop that danced haphazardly. He imagined it had been a change of the wind, but it struck him as odd that the waves would be so active this close to shore. The wind must have been just right to blow them that way. It was mid-gray now with the coming light, but with the storm still blowing as it was, he couldn't make out much farther than fifty yards.

He needed to do a more thorough check of the ice. Stopping at his gear, he pulled the sledge over next to the chair and looped some of the drawcords around the legs of the chair to keep the wind, or the next big fish, from pulling it too far. He checked the rod. It was sufficiently wedged into the chair to stay put, and the bail was locked. Satisfied, he tucked the rest of his gear away into the sledge or near it and then took his bearings off the chair, the hole, and his quickly disappearing footprints that led to open water. Turning toward his memory of shore, he cinched his coat and set his hood, for he was now fully facing the wind. It felt stronger this way, and he realized that the storm was still blowing with as much force as it had earlier in the night, possibly more. He'd found some refuge in sitting and hunching against it. But with it full in his face, walking against it, he was reminded of its strength. He'd do a quick circuit to shore to check on things, then get back to the comparative comfort of the chair.

Leaning into the wind, he stepped away from his gear. He felt mired walking into the wind. He was used to moving slow with his joints and his back and his loneliness, but fighting such a foe is something else, much more tiring. The wind doesn't care, of course, but it was an adversary nonetheless, and he found himself silently cursing it as he leaned against it. With a gust, his hood filled with snow, little frozen crystals grinding like cold salt. He cinched it more, but cold still somehow found its way in with each burst of wind. He trudged on. Though he'd set up relatively close to shore on the ice pack, the walk back took longer than he'd expected. The ice shouldn't have shuddered like that, and his mind was playing out scenarios, possibilities.

With the wind and his walking, he no longer heard the sounds of the ice. That calmed him some. Not that the sounds really worried him. It was the shaking. He'd never been in an earthquake, but he imagined that's what it was like, having the ground under your feet suddenly move. How disorienting. Ice is naturally unstable. Here it gets so stable that it's easy to forget. *We all forget it*, he thought, *even me.* He stopped in his tracks and looked down at the solid white beneath his feet. Every year, huts, snow machines, cars—and the men and women inside them—ended up falling through the ice because they forgot. How easy it was. One moment, you're standing on something solid and immovable. And the next, your heart is in your throat, and you feel helpless as the ground beneath you crumbles.

He palmed the ice picks dangling from the strings over his shoulders and gripped their reassuring handles. A recurring image flashed in his mind: tendrils of oil on dark water, shivering gasps, and uncovered fingers clawing at crumbling ice. His eyes shut hard against it, and his breath faltered. He shook his head, willed it away, and imagined himself suddenly over open water. He imagined the float of things in the unexpected absence of a firm surface beneath, in the moment before it all wrapped around him and he was sealed in unending cold.

He pushed the thought aside and stepped once again into the white.

Making his way toward the memory of shore, he was surprised to find that the wind didn't calm. Usually, it waned the closer he got to the cliffs and the trees of the shoreline. Maybe he was out farther than he thought, and the wind was holding him back more than he'd expected. He was surprised but not worried.

In a few steps, he found something that did worry him: the sound of waves.

Soon, an ice edge came into view where he thought the shore should have been. His chest tightened, and he felt a ball at the base of his throat. There was pack ice, a break, and then water. It looked like the edge near his gear. It didn't make sense. He'd been walking in the direction of shore, for more than a short while, and now there was this edge of open water. It didn't fit his mental map. It didn't fit.

He stood there, a bit back from the edge, stuck. His mind turned over possibilities. The ice gave nothing away, no clues, though he checked for them. He stepped left, then right, as if a shift in perspective might yield the truth. The smooth surface and bits of snow were like a blank parchment. He stood there a long while. This was wrong, but how wrong? He thought he'd walked true, but maybe with the wind, he'd turned. That certainly happens in wind and snow. It doesn't take much reading of mountaineers in the snowpack to find stories of lost climbers in the blank of winter. They use poles and branches and markers to leave a path behind them, things that are harder to bury in snow or blow away in a gale. But he'd left nothing, and his footprints were long gone. He could have been correctly retracing his steps, but that would mean the pack had broken free. That wouldn't have happened. And if it had . . .

He interrupted himself to envision a different, more likely scenario. He'd gotten turned around in the snow and the wind and looped back on himself to some other section of ice. He thought of how big the pack might be, how far off track he must have been. Lost people often walk in circles. He'd probably looped. But he knew if he followed the ice edge, he'd either find the shore or his sledge and spot, and he could start back to find the other once more.

He looked out at the water in front of him, at the splashing, dark, frigid Lake Superior, and tried to divine where he was, how he had become so suddenly lost.

He turned to follow the edge of the pack and began walking.

CHAPTER SEVEN

He turned a map in his mind. It showed the rough edge of shore, from that gentle slope near the creek to the steep cliffs near Leif Erikson Park and the drops to the flats and the brewhouse beyond. The pack couldn't be more than a couple miles long and maybe half a mile wide. If he followed the edge, he'd end up at shore soon enough. Still, it didn't give him much confidence. He felt disoriented. Of course he did, that's what being lost is. But it's much more than losing your bearings. It's a sense of being. He had a sense of foreboding, of doom, and he suddenly felt hot in the frigid wind. His stomach tensed, and his bones ached. But he'd spent a lifetime dulling his emotions, flattening his response, muting himself against pain and loss, because it was easier than feeling. So he channeled that energy into numbing, pushed his nervousness to the pit of his stomach.

He trudged on along the edge of the ice pack. Just beyond, the water danced and riffled with the wind. *It's funny,* he thought, *to be where water meets ice. It's in the air we breathe, the liquid we drink, and the surface I'm walking on.* The boundary between them, the subtle boundary that he could see all around him, made him feel like he was balanced precariously between worlds. Lapping water could either add layers to the ice or break it down. It was all about the conditions, the temperature. Such a subtle thing, to shift from one to the other. And yet, it could change everything.

Those waves, he thought, *if they start rolling more, might break up the floe.*

That made him think of his gear. It was close to the edge but not at the edge. It might be safe from bits breaking off, but cracks in the pack were something else. Those could go from one end to the other or break off vast fields of ice. Those could turn your world around in a hurry. There wasn't much to do about it, though, other than keep on. So, he followed the line where the ice met the water, and for now, it held fast.

In his walk along the pack, he observed that it was firm, and the edge was intact all around. After leaving untold steps behind him, he found a sharp curve and took a tight turn to the left, which surprised him. He hadn't realized how turned around he was. He rotated the map in his mind, held it up in front of him, switched imaginary hands, and tilted it back and forth. Nothing matched. He was looking at something entirely different. He scoffed, spat into the water, and suddenly realized how dry his mouth was. *Stop thinking and just keep the water on your right,* he thought, *and it'll take you to one or the other.* It was a funny thing, a sharp turn. He imagined the corner of ice where he stood, somewhere offshore, a curving line of steps looping back and forth on itself in his wake. He looked at the curve, at the anomaly of the edge, a little bump in the pack.

Water on the right. He shifted his coat, opened a zipper to vent his body heat, adjusted his hood to keep out the drift, and trudged on.

The pack was long and narrow, and by the time he'd walked the entirety of the edge, to the point at the far end and back again, the muted glow of the sun was already well on its way back to the horizon. He couldn't find the sun in the clouds, couldn't put it in front of him to find west, but the quality of the light had changed. It was dimmer but also took more of a slant.

When little spots of darkness appeared on the ice and he realized he had found his gear, he felt relief wash over him like a warm shower, and that ball in his gut disappeared. He was no longer lost. He knew where he was. His gear was there, his rod and his sledge and the augered hole. It had taken him until well past noon to find it, but there it was. He was no longer lost. He knew where he was on the ice. He'd been turned around, sure, but he'd gotten to this spot on his own, the spot he knew, and he just needed to head out the other direction next time and get back to shore.

The wind and the cold have a way of pulling the water from your bones, and he felt it. He was thirsty. He worked the strings on the sledge with his heavy mitts and clumsy fingers, then peeled back the layers of the sledge liner to find his water bottle. It was frozen solid. Unzipping his jacket, he slid the bottle into a pocket in the warm interior and closed the zipper. Even through the weave of his sweater, the bottle burned his skin with cold. Still thirsty, he knelt down to the hole he'd drilled earlier. It was covered with a thin rime of ice. He tapped it with his mitt, and it cracked easily. Taking his hand from his mitt, he reached down into the cold water and cupped small handfuls of Lake Superior up to his lips, slurping it down. His lips were dry, and the chill of the water was refreshing in his throat. There's a timer out there in the cold, measuring how long until frostbite starts to set in. It varies based on the wind and the cold, but Hugh estimated it to be only a few minutes, with how bitter it was. The timer starts when your skin is exposed, runs faster with the wet, and when it runs out, you're off on a bad run toward dead tissue and a lifetime of cold. Or worse. His thirst sated, his hand was drifting from aching to numb. He shook off the excess water, wiped it on his pants, and slid it back into the protection of his mitt.

His hand would be fine, he thought. It hadn't been out long, and it had been in the comparative warmth of the water. But it ached nonetheless, and he swung it to get the blood flowing. No, he hadn't let it out too long. But it wouldn't take much more. It was colder than he'd thought. *Never mind three minutes*, he thought, *more like one.* He felt the ache ebb from his fingers, felt the throb as blood from his core thumped in his palm and across the back of his hand and under his nails.

His chair had tipped, and he righted it, still swinging the cold hand as he sat down. He looked at the fishing pole still wedged into the legs of the chair. The line had been in the water while he was wandering on the ice, and he hoped that the tip of the chair meant that a fish had taken the hook. The line was taut to the hole, but when he pulled at the rod, he felt only the weight of the lure and the whoosh of water along the line, as if he were trolling. He placed it back in the legs of the chair, where it would be secure, and sat back to think.

He wasn't sure if he'd try for another scouting mission, but he did need to rest, to think. Just like the tip of the chair, it must have been the wind that had turned him around. He must have walked and turned from the wind, which had put him on a curved course back to the edge of the pack. It was so preposterous, he thought, to turn so far off course, but it was the only acceptable answer. He wondered if the same thing would happen again if he struck out to look. He wondered, too, if there was any worth in trying. He hardly remembered why he'd gone in the first place. That's when he remembered the crack—the thump and the shudder of the ice. This felt like lead in his stomach, a heaviness that came and wouldn't leave. He stumbled around his justifications and plausible scenarios, but the weight wouldn't go. Something was wrong. He was lost, or at least turned around enough to become lost, even though he'd found his gear again. What if he struck out once more, only to lose his way again, and this time he didn't find his equipment? Something was off. He thought about the value in searching again, of looking for . . . *the shore?* That was stupid—the shore was just behind him. He'd just gotten turned around last time. It would be there.

But how had he gotten lost? Maybe it would have made sense over the course of miles of walking, but he'd hardly walked that far. So how had he been so turned around? As he sat in the cold, staring at the blank, he began to sweat. His parka and mitts and hat suddenly felt hot, oppressive. He pulled at his scarf, opened zippers, turned left and right, and looked behind him. It was still impossible to see very far at all, and nothing more was revealed to him. The lead in his belly was hot now too, heavy and hot. He wanted to be rid of it, but it just kept on burning. He took deep breaths, in through his nose and out through his mouth, big puffs of steam that the wind slapped away.

He couldn't risk losing his gear. Not only was it necessary for him to do what he'd come out there to do, but it had his emergency supplies. The only way to be sure not to lose it was to bring it with him. Still, he'd been grounded by finding it again, so he risked losing that feeling of knowing. But he decided it would be better to become lost with his gear than to be lost without it. And besides, the hole in the ice would be there, so if he stood in this spot again, he'd know it.

Decision made, he pulled the rod from the chair and reeled in the line. It went slow now that he was motivated to move, felt like the line might never spool back on the reel. Still, he forced himself to do it smoothly and methodically all the same. There's nothing worse than reeling frantically. The line reflects how you feel, shows you're undone in curls and tangles. But he wasn't undone. Nope. No, he was good. He wasn't out of it yet. His gut burned, but he knew what he was doing, knew to do it slowly and methodically.

Finally, the little curl of cisco and the lure plopped out of the water, and he slid his hand from the mitt once more. His fingers delicately picked the jig from where it dangled, his huge knuckles obscuring the little thing, and he tucked the hook into the metal next to the eyelet on the rod and reeled in the slack on the line so the hook held fast. He tucked his hand back into the mitt and set the rod in the sledge. He set the frying pan in the sledge too, as deep as he could, as ballast. His catch, the trout, was now frozen solid, and he placed it like cordwood next to the pan, the meat clinking against the metal. He collapsed the chair and set it next to the frying pan. Last in was the auger, and he hid that and everything else with the sledge cover and then cinched it tight. He took the shovel and laced it under the lashing cord and pulled at the knots until the shovel and the bundle below it were secure. When he pulled at the tow line on the sledge, the whole thing moved like the enormous hull of a laker filled with ore.

He was ready to head for shore to check the ice. He'd find it, then scout for another spot to auger and fish. His lure had gone for nearly an hour without so much as a nibble. This was a dry hole now anyway.

The sense of purpose and action cooled the hot lead in his stomach, but the weight remained. So much yet undone. He turned and walked toward shore once more, the sledge dutifully following behind him, erasing what tracks he made as he went.

CHAPTER EIGHT

As he walked away from his fishing hole, he waited for a sense of calm that never came. He'd hoped that he might regain some sense of grounding and orientation. But with each step back toward shore, he felt more and more like he was losing his grip on reality. He imagined what he was doing in the abstract. He was leaving a known place to go back to a known place to confirm he knew where he was. That was it, wasn't it? But if he knew both of these places, why would he need to confirm their existence?

The lead in his stomach returned. It was heavy and it burned.

He leaned further into the work of pulling the sledge. It wasn't usually hard, but again the wind seemed to hold him back with each step. Still, he opened his jacket to vent the heat building inside. The sledge itself slid confidently on, its runners smooth on the ice and snow.

It wasn't a long walk, but the turmoil in his mind made it drag. As he went, he concentrated on a straight path, an unwavering course. He had no compass with him, but he had his bearings, or so he thought, and he had his sledge now to point out if he turned sharply. Like a train car lagging behind in a bend, it would stay true even if he wavered, even if only for a moment. He looked back at it now and found it as straight as ever, and in his mind, he could picture tracks all the way back to the fishing hole. Soon he would be standing on the stone of the point.

The wind and the snow made a mess of things, and he could barely see a hundred feet ahead. When the edge came into view, he first thought it a mirage, a deep gray line in the muted white and gray of his existence. But it grew sharper as he approached, and the heavy feeling spread to his chest. He approached dangerously close to the edge to confirm that it was truly there.

It should have been shore. He'd been sure of it. He stood now, his shoulders drooped, the line of the sledge dangling from one hand. He stared at the ice, listened to the wind and now the lapping of waves near the toes of his mukluks. He stared at it as if to will it to be different. His gaze was unblinking. His mouth was tight in a firm line, his jaw muscles pulling grooves in his skin and his teeth creaking from pressure.

His confidence cracked with the edge of the ice, and now he stood there, staring out, his heart thumping loud and quick in his chest as his throat tightened.

What in damnation? Where's my goddamn shore? His rational mind was trying to make sense of it, but the rawness of his emotions was eroding the other part of his mind. He worked to pull his thoughts together, but it was like backpedaling in sand, barely keeping up. That frantic part of him was overcoming the rational part, and it offered him all the reasons he could be wrong about what he was looking at. *Maybe we arced to the side. Maybe you're just an old coot and can't walk in a straight line anymore.* Everything pointed to the wind and snow and ice throwing him off. He was on the wrong part of the pack. His breathing was shaky, and he made a feeble attempt to slow it, to even it out, to use it to calm the booming in his chest.

He had to accept that he was lost because the alternative was too unbearable. To be adrift on the pack in the void of the lake would be a solitary, slow execution.

He had to be lost. He took comfort in the thought that he was lost. It was a manageable thing. To be lost is to have a starting point and a goal but not to know where you are in between them. There are boundaries to it, an opportunity for containment of the situation. Not so if he were adrift. No, he was lost on the pack. He was a stupid old man who had gotten turned around. How could he be so stupid? He felt some relief at the self-flagellation. It was familiar territory for him, and as he continued to convince himself, he felt a calm temper the thump of his heart and steady his breath. But there was a tightness that would not go away. It stuck somewhere near his clavicle and branched down along his ribs. There was probably truth in that feeling, but he worked now to ignore it.

You are lost on the ice, he told himself, *so you have to find your way back.*

He turned now to the right and started along the edge of the pack. He would loop around until he found shore. There were plenty of cliffs nearby, but he would gladly take an insurmountable cliff. Oh, the joy he would feel if he reached a cliff he could not climb. He could skirt around them easily. He would find shore and climb up it, and he would be off the pack. He would walk up the hill toward home, past the still-quiet houses, and find his alley and his garage. The bare bulb would be bright after such dark and gray, and he would leave all his things in the sledge and go inside. He would leave piles of clothing and boots in a path from the side door to the kitchen, and he would leave too many layers on, and he would bask in the warmth of sweater and hat in a warm home and then the scald of hot water in the shower, and he would think about how scared he had been and how good it was to be home.

But that daydream made the air around him even colder. It left an emptiness in him, a hollow spot filled with worry. All around was white and gray of ice and snow and cloud and the churning water of Lake Superior. He thought of how empty everything was, how stark, and he realized that he could return to this very spot and not realize he'd been there before. He had to mark it somehow.

He stopped, and the sledge scooted to a halt behind him. He stood there for a minute and thought through how he could mark it. He could leave something behind, but he felt compelled now to keep his things with him. He had the axe and could hack marks in the ice, but those could fill with snow or be easy to miss. He finally settled on using the auger. He would make two holes, one next to the other. There would be these two holes, at this spot, and his previous hole on the other side. That would be clear.

He undid the cord on the sledge and lifted the auger from where it sat below. As before, he set it carefully on the ice and began turning the handles. The work was slow at first, but his arms soon warmed from the effort, and that pleased him in the cold. Finally, the auger broke through, and the splash of water sloshing from the hole told him it was done. He repeated the process just a foot away from the first. With this one, he felt his muscles cramping, needed to pause to catch his breath. When he finished, he would take a drink from the water bottle if it had thawed. The burn of his muscles was uncomfortable, but he got through before they seized up entirely, and he was happy for that. He dragged the auger back to the sledge and tucked it back in its place before finding the bottle among his many layers. It was partially thawed, and he was able to take several sips. Unzipping his parka, he put the bottle back inside to continue to melt. It was uncomfortable, but he needed to be able to drink. Done, he shut the sledge and secured the lashing before rising to his feet to strike out once again along the edge of the pack.

CHAPTER NINE

With open water to his left and the ice pack to his right, he trudged on through the blowing gray and white. The inky dark of Lake Superior water danced wildly and now made him uneasy. It felt heavy, like there was more gravity than before and it might pull him in if he simply got too close to it. His progress was steady. His breathing was heavy under the strain of the sledge and the cold and the worry. His stomach still held the mass of lead, and though he was now working toward something, it still glowed red with heat.

A gust of wind threw snow into his hood, and he flinched away from the sudden blast. He stood there, huddled against it for a moment until the gust subsided. It was replaced by the constant whip and scream of the heavy winds. Later in the day now, the light was still dim as the winter storm clouds veiled the sun and falling, blowing snow filtered it even more. The low light and the thick weather made it feel like he was suspended in twilight, a gray in-between world. It also made seeing all the more difficult. The ice blended with the horizon, which blended with the sky. The only solid things were his sledge behind him and the roiling water off to his left. These were dark shadows among the gray.

His pilgrimage took him a long time. He was being methodical, but he was also growing tired. Despite the cold, his parka hung open to vent the heat from his exertion. He had to pace himself to keep up what was left of his energy. Many younger fishermen push and push and use up everything they have by going fast. What he'd come to know over time is that you can do anything if you do it slowly. To rush through is to use up what you have quickly. If he went slowly, he knew he could keep up his pace and keep some semblance of calm. Regardless of the pace, the spur of worry pushed him to keep walking until he found land or his augered holes, no matter how tired he got.

He let the ice edge guide him and kept walking until, rounding a wide bend, he realized he had been there before. He paused and surveyed the area, turning the maps in his mind. When one of them matched, he realized he'd found the edge ice from near his first fishing hole. He knew the opening itself would be a fair way in from the edge. Finding a contour of ice he recognized, he turned and found the hole without issue. It had iced over again. Removing his water bottle from his parka, he found it was only slightly more melted than before. He drank the ice melt from the bottle and broke the thin layer covering the hole with his boot before bending down with the bottle to dip it full of cold Lake Superior water. Before rising, he drank several full sips from the bottle, then filled it again to the brim. He replaced the cap, turned it tight, and tucked it safely back into his parka.

He'd tasked himself with following the edge to his old hole or land, whichever came first, and if the hole came first, to continue along again until he found land or the double holes. It wasn't complicated, and it was doable. If he started to think too much on what it meant that he'd found the hole instead of land, he might unravel.

He wasted no time. Standing, he turned from the hole and set off once more. He kept the dancing waves to his left and the gray emptiness to his right. One foot and then the other.

The walk went slowly and was marked only by the tight curve at the corner halfway between the two places he'd drilled. He remembered that, too, which both reassured him and added more dread. Still, he pushed the depth of his worry away until it could be confirmed beyond doubt.

The storm continued. Gray light was awash with thick, blowing snowfall. It seemed to fall directly into the water, as if the water weren't even there or the snow transmuted instantly from crystal to liquid as it touched the water. On the ice, it skittered across the surface in a layer like steam. Visibility was still limited but had lifted to maybe 150 feet. It wasn't enough to change the view, but it did extend the line of ice edge that he could see and the empty gray on either side.

When the pair of augered holes began to appear at the edge of the whiteout, he was filled again with the sense of knowing where he was. And with that, came the tightening of dread. Seeing them would confirm it, but still, he suspected—hoped—it was a mirage. He quickened his pace and curved toward them, the two dots growing from the distance until he reached them and dropped to his hands and knees, looking through them like they were portholes into another world. He heard his heart thumping through the down of his insulation layer and the shell of his parka, and he stared at the inky dark, wishing it showed something more than those empty depths.

What came surprised him. He thought of Sarah.

His memory of his wife was so limited now, a handful of freeze-frames that no longer seemed like they came from his own lifetime—the recollection of a ghost.

She was standing at the kitchen sink, a pale-pink-and-blue apron draped over her neck, blue ties cinched in a bow at the small of her back. She worked at a pile of dishes, the dim light above casting her back in blue shadow. Her movements were fluid and easy, her focus on her task, and on him. Her neck would curve and they would banter. The dishes got done. Or interrupted . . .

Then in the water, he saw that neck. It was her, and wrong. She was ashen. Her jaw slack, open, motionless. Frozen in a gasp. Sinking slowly away. He felt the pull on his own body, as if he would be ripped through into the cold below.

He pushed away, closed his eyes hard, tears forced out between the lids. When he opened them, all he saw was the grotesque mask of a terrified old man. And he wept.

He was exhausted. From the day, the months, the years alone. And the memory. All of it exhausting.

He hadn't started that way—he'd slowly become a sour shell over years. Years of loss turned to pessimism and doubt, to years of shuttered windows. Things had been better. He'd overcome the stark emptiness of his childhood and made a family. But that dream had been taken from him. It was all he could manage to go on, to start and finish each day as the husk of himself. None of it had happened to him—it had happened around him. But it had formed him just the same, molded him into a husk of his current self—a gaunt old man.

But what he saw most was regret. He saw echoes of so many moments and decisions he wished he had done differently. From his parents, to his children and his wife, his interactions with them were now a collection of moments in the past, moments he'd fumbled and could no longer change. He stood, looked on as if hoping that he would wake up, that this was a terrible dream.

But staring down through the hole in the ice, he felt the cold, the bitterness of his perception, and there was no other world to see but that of the fish below. This wasn't a dream. There was simply the cold gray where he now stood. The muted emptiness where he was alone on an ice floe, afloat and drifting on the great inland sea of Lake Superior. He imagined the view from above, as if floating over himself, looking down at the sad heap of parka. Then his perspective slowly rose so that he could see both himself and the ice edge, and then the curving round of the edge of the pack, and then the far edge with the other hole. It kept rising so he could see the whole pack, with the gentle curve to the left, and the sharp corner to the right. All surrounded by water. He kept rising, and the ice shrank as the lake grew, until the floe was but one dot of many in the great emptiness of the lake. The shore was impossibly far, and as it appeared, the vision broke, and he saw the colorless static of the storm and the ice.

A buzz began in his head, like bees nesting in the walls. He felt them as much as heard them, and they grew with a heavy heat that filled up from the bottom of his stomach and rose to a deep flush in his cheeks. With them came a quickening of breath. The realization was physically painful, and he felt ill. As the buzzing increased, the sounds of the ice and wind around him dimmed until all he heard was the din of the whole hive between his ears, interrupted only by the heavy whomp of his heart beating faster and faster in his chest. He suddenly wished for someone else. Anyone. Either as a companion to his misery or as a spectator. Someone who knew his situation. He would be forgotten, his demise a cruel mystery. He felt his body giving way, the loosening of his leg muscles, the buckling of joints—as if burning from tremendous heat despite the frozen world around him. His knees bent and he lowered, down, down to the ice, his head and hands coming to rest on the cold, hard ice as his chest heaved and his face burned with the terror of his realization.

His end was set, a clock ticking—a future now certain and condensed, even more so than a diagnosis. He had days, or maybe hours.

This would be his death. It would be slow and agonizing and alone.

He sat up, and his eyes fixed on the muted emptiness in front of him. His eyes were wide. His mittened hands were on the ice, as if trying to hold together the surface beneath. His back heaved with the quickening breath and his mouth twisted, jaw opening as if pulled apart. His breathing grew louder, overpowering the wind. His vision of emptiness blurred. The crescendo of his breathing suddenly stopped with one enormous inhale. It came out in a terrible yell, a cry that might rend the ice in two. That's what he felt was happening to him. He was coming apart. But it was more than the silence of the day that was breaking. It was the silence of years. It poured out like the breaking of a dam. Again and again until he had nothing left, and then his body was racked with uncontrollable coughing. It seized his torso as if he were being electrified, the air squeezed from his lungs. When it finally subsided, he slumped over on the ice in a panting heap.

He was lost, adrift, alone. He had finally broken the silence.

PART II

CHAPTER TEN

Hugh stayed slumped on the ice for what seemed like a very long time.

His sobs slowly calmed until his back rose with each steady breath and fell with each quick exhale. He felt that rise and fall and began to perceive the movement of the ice. It was so subtle—a constant, steady motion, and the murmur of water chopping against it. And he heard the twang of straining ice too, which bothered him. It reminded him that he was kneeling on a brittle surface.

That realization brought him back to the present, and his mind snapped to attention. He had to figure out his options.

With the wind, shouts for help would just scatter. Besides, there wasn't anyone to hear them. There was no one out in this awful weather but him. No one for who knew how many miles. He could make as much noise as he wanted, and it wouldn't make a lick of difference. He thought of his other options for signaling, other ways to show that he needed help. Thinking through the contents of his sledge, he came up with nothing of value, short of exploding the gas tank of his stove. But that would only be useful if someone was already looking.

That's just the problem, he thought. No one would be looking for him. No one knew he was there. He hadn't told anyone he'd be out. Hadn't told a neighbor. He didn't work, so there'd be no Monday-morning call that he hadn't shown. Even if someone checked on him, they would only know that he was out of the house. *Maybe they'd look in the garbage,* he thought, *find the cisco entrails and put two and two together.* That was wishful thinking. No one was going to look. No one cared.

And that filled him with an emptiness that was bigger than him.

No one cared that he was out here. Why would they? He was a sad old man who'd screwed up the little grace he'd gotten and who'd put himself in this situation on his own. No one to blame but himself. God may have laid the trap and sprung the latch, but it was his own damn fault. And damnit if this wasn't how he was going to go. His self-pity waned as he shifted toward anger. It was perhaps better, though. Anger might motivate him. Feeling sorry for himself might lead him to the ice edge and into the water of his own accord, but frustration might lead him to action.

He thought through his journey down, his walk along the streets, and his walk through the neighborhood. No one would have seen him. And though his feet and the pulk had left a mighty strong trail, that trail would already be gone, filled with drifts of snow. He was already like a ghost, even if he hadn't become one yet. Would he know when it happened? Would he be aware of the end of the one thing and the beginning of the other? Or would he simply drift off to sleep one moment and rise again, doomed to his purgatory on the cold emptiness? He imagined the unending freeze, the wind, the flatness. It scared him. If he ever slept, he might never wake.

He tried to imagine how far out he might be now, how far from shore. *How fast am I going?* If it was a slow drift, he would have floated past the houses and apartments at the bottom of Twenty-First. Squinting into the distance, he imagined what might be the shore, could see them in his mind's eye, a set of tall town houses built right along the lake, standing like a wall of lighthouses. They might as well be on the other side of the earth. He couldn't swim, couldn't yell, and couldn't see them. They were on another planet. But he could be far beyond them now, somewhere out in the middle of the saltless sea.

He thought of his cell phone on the kitchen counter, plugged into the wall. That's where it lived, always with its charger. He was afraid to let the battery run down at all, for fear that the bars would drop like a stone and it would die when he needed it. And if that could happen at home, it was sure to happen out in the cold. No, the battery was full, but that didn't do him much good. The phone was not in his pocket. Not in the sledge. Not with him where he could use it to dial his neighbor or his daughter or 911. Instead, it sat in the kitchen, battery full and ready.

He thought of his schedule, empty as it was, for anything that might raise suspicion as to his whereabouts. This, too, led nowhere. It was now Saturday, and he had no plans. Same as Sunday: nothing. Come Monday morning, though, he had an appointment with his oncologist. That would be the first thing he'd miss. It wouldn't be likely, though, for them to worry too much about a missed appointment. He'd get a call later asking to reschedule, and it would ring through to that cell phone on the counter. They wouldn't be calling 911 for a no-show. No one would go to his house. He was nervous about that appointment anyway, wasn't looking forward to hearing about how far it had spread by now. He scoffed at how it had worried him. Whatever his prognosis, it couldn't touch the lethality and lonely demise he now faced here on the ice. How trivial it had all been, the talk of years and months. How ridiculous it seemed to him now that he realized he was going to die on the ice or in the water. He would probably be dead before he even missed his appointment. He laughed, more like a sputter, and it launched him into a spasming cough that bent him forward with stabs of pain in his ribs. He coughed until the air was all gone, and he stayed curled there like a wilted flower until his breath slowly returned. He wiped the tears from his eyes before they froze, and looked out again at the emptiness.

How long would the pack last? *That depends on the weather*, he thought, *the action of the waves, and the temperature.* If the wind calmed and the cold stayed, the pack could freeze up again, and he'd have a clear path to somewhere. But that was wishful thinking. He remembered the forecast in the paper from the day before. It showed the cold would stay, but so would the wind. Gale warnings through the weekend and into the week. Superior would be blowing big waves out to the east. At least that's what they'd said. And that's what he saw written in the gloom too. No end in sight. Except his own.

Hugh figured that he was on a dwindling sheet, which would continue to get smaller as he drifted. He thought through his gear for anything that could help with navigation. He had no map, no compass, or crude navigating tools either. If the stars were out, he could look at them, but he'd never learned to navigate by them, just to look and wonder at the abstractness of Orion and the Ursas and the Dipper. That wasn't much help now. He thought back to nautical books he'd read and some of the tricks that sailors used, some of the techniques. The best he could think was something along the lines of tracking his speed by knots playing out in a rope. But he had nothing to base it on to link it to real distance or usefulness. And besides, he didn't actually know where he was or how long he'd been drifting. He imagined he was only creeping along, but for how long? How far? With the wind, he guessed that the creep could actually have some decent speed over hours or days.

He imagined Lake Superior again from above, this time viewing its vastness from space. That was almost easier to wrap his head around. From space, it's bounded by the shoreline; there are the edges that form the shape of a wolf's head, the ears to the northeast, the snout pointing southwest, and the eye of Isle Royale near the northwest corner. It's something you can grasp. But looking out on that great expanse from shore, and seeing nothing but water, looking out at an ocean that spans beyond what you can see? That's more than you can imagine. That's endless. Its scale gets lost on that satellite image. But on the ground, and on the water, it's immense. Even from the shore in Duluth, at its narrowest points, it looks like it will never end, like a great void that might just pull you in if you're not paying attention. Was that him? Had he let his guard down, stopped paying attention, and fallen prey to the void?

He suddenly felt so small. And his ice pack felt like a tiny raft. He felt the distance of far shores and the distance of his home like a pang. Maybe it was regret, maybe fear. Whatever it was, it was primal. He was lost, and it pulled at an elemental feeling. He felt so disconnected, and his body knew that was wrong. It was a state he wasn't supposed to be in. It clawed at him. But there was nothing he could do. He was adrift, at the whim of the water and ice.

CHAPTER ELEVEN

The storm continued into evening.

Hugh remained on his knees, staring at where the shore once was, at the static of snow and wind and the empty lake beyond the ice edge. His mind was frozen. He felt glued down. He should have thrown another line or two in while he waited, but it felt wrong to fish. What for? Was he going to bring it home? He might never be home again. What good would a fish be? But then, another thought again crossed his mind—darker, in some ways, than never returning. *How long will I be out here?* he thought. He was imagining the purgatory of the living, that his raft and his mortal shell might, in fact, last longer than he expected.

As he looked at the ice around him now, it suddenly felt silent and empty in a way that it hadn't before. The noise of his thoughts had blocked out the wind and the water, but the quiet too. Now, he was confronted with the vastness around him. Visibility had improved slightly, and he could see the jerky edge of the ice as it curved away from him, the dark gloss of snowless ice, and the bright spots of snow upon it. He heard the wind rise and fall, and the slap of water on ice all around.

What a boat to be on, he thought, *this slab of ice.*

He thought back to the ice cracking. When had it happened? Was it that thunk of ice he'd heard? He imagined if he'd reacted instead of simply sitting there. What would have happened if he'd gotten up and left all his gear out there on the ice and run toward shore? Maybe he could have gotten close enough to step back to safety or gotten out in a quick swim. If he'd gotten up and realized what had happened, maybe he could have yelled for help while he was still close enough to be heard. But he hadn't done that. He'd sat and fished. And the gap had grown.

The thought of his complacency ached in him now and he shouted in a throat-burning roar. He yelled until all the air left him and he was empty again. It threw him into a spasm of coughing once more, and then he began to cry, two gasping sobs, followed by another half roar, more painful coughing, and more tears. They rolled down his cheeks and fell to the snow. He dropped his face to the ice and beat at it with his mitts.

He sat there for a long time. Long enough for the sun to finish its course over the earth and to dip once again toward the horizon, long enough to drift miles farther out into the lake. He was in a daze, not really there, frozen in time.

He sat there long enough for the storm to clear. He saw it in the liminal light, sat in awe of the sudden change, whipped by wind. One minute, the thick pall that had surrounded him peeled back, fingers of the storm, the last tendrils of cloud like claws dragging behind. Then, it was a wall behind him, the world suddenly open. He watched, mouth agape at the release.

He could suddenly see clear, dim skies overhead and the lake becoming visible all around him, except for the receding wall of white like a sandstorm on this water desert. He could see the entire ice pack now, the vastness of it, and how small it was in the big water that surrounded it. The horizon was visible now, and all around was the thin transition of sky to water, of endlessness. All but one direction, where he made out the faintest hint of shore: a thin line. Or was it more ice? He couldn't quite tell, but in either case, he'd drifted far and was headed out to more open water. The drift was inevitable. The visibility did give him an idea. If he could see the shore, the shore could potentially see a signal. Maybe a flash, or a column of smoke?

Without getting up, he pulled his pulk alongside and untied the cover. The fish was on top like a sculpture, frozen solid. It looked like a perfect wall mount, but for its clouded eyes. He scoffed at it. He'd come to the ice for the fish, and now he was lost. The fish looked smaller now too, inconsequential. He thought how easy it was to see the uselessness of a thing after it brought you ruin. Before that, it could mean the world to you. He picked the fish up by the tail and tossed it out of the pulk. It clunked like heavy glass on the ice.

He peeled back the contents of the pulk, looking for things that might burn or pop and things that might make heavy smoke. He found the stove and set it next to him. Next, he found his sleeping bag. He paused as he considered it. It would certainly burn and, he imagined, give a plume of heavy smoke. But burning it seemed like a hopeless plea, a last-ditch effort that would lead to his salvation or be a nail in his coffin. There was no knowing if anyone would even see, if this signal would work, and how long he would be on the ice either way. And with night coming, he would need the bag in order to see morning. He had to find something less necessary. The fishing gear wouldn't burn, nor the chair, other than its small patch of fabric strung between the metal bars. He found the canvas tarp and again considered whether it would be better used for a survival shelter or a signal device.

No one is looking, he thought. *No one is looking for me.*

There was nothing so useless that he could burn it without likely sealing his fate sometime in the near future. And the likelihood of a fire bringing help was so low, he couldn't justify it. If a plane went over, he imagined, that might be different. If there was a plane or a person looking, he might burn the whole lot. That was something else entirely. That would be people looking for him, asking for a signal. But lighting a fire for someone on shore to spot by chance? It would be fruitless, a waste.

How could he show someone he was there without destroying anything?

There were his spoons, a couple tucked away in his tackle box. He could use the big shiny piece of metal as a crude signal mirror. He thought about spelling *help* out on the ice. He could wrangle that together with some of his things, could even use the auger to carve it out in dots if he wanted. But someone would have to be looking at it, be looking for him, for it to help. Everything pointed to the same problem: Someone needed to be trying to find him.

He looked out at the ice pack. It was huge, stretched out in a pattern of white and shine, motionless against the backdrop of dark, shimmering water around it.

It reminded him of when he was a child, standing out in a field of wheat kissed gold by afternoon sun. It was a memory that he'd forgotten, repressed perhaps, but it came clearly now, resurrected from the deep of his subconscious. He was playing hide-and-seek, looking for a hiding spot. He was out of breath, searching the field for anything out of the ordinary. He checked behind him. No one there yet. So he ventured further. He'd go to the middle, where the wheat was tallest, and hide there. The wheat bent as he waded in, the stems singing against one another. The field was bigger than he'd thought, and reaching the middle took some time. Hunkered down there, he felt almost cozy. Beginning to hear voices, he crouched down until he was under the wheat, feeling like he was underwater.

He stayed there as the voices rose and fell and then gave way to silence. His hiding spot was so good they couldn't find him. He waited. And while he waited, the sun slowly set, and the field grew cold. He curled up against the cold and waited. He was nervous. Were his friends still looking for him? He suddenly felt forgotten, assumed he had been, because otherwise they'd have been out looking for him, yelling his name. How could they forget him? When would they remember him? He knew he shouldn't leave his spot, had to stay to wait to be found. He waited as the cold deepened. As he lay there in the dark, he tried not to let his imagination fill the shadows with things scarier than the reality of being lost, with monsters and bad people.

Eventually, after stars had long painted the sky, he heard voices, noticed the dance of flashlight beams across the wheat. Had his friends finally come to find him? He waited. The lights brightened and then finally landed on his curled little form. Behind them were a man and a woman, dressed all in brown: dark-brown stripes down the sides of their khaki legs and thick brown coats with sparkling sheriff's badges at the breast. The man spoke calmly, called him by his name, and wrapped him in his coat. He picked him up and carried him back through the field and the woods to his waiting truck. The inside of the truck was warm and smelled of summer sun and musty gear. His friends were gone, but the deputy told him that when he hadn't appeared at sundown, they'd told their parents, who'd gone out looking in the dark. They'd called 911.

The deputy pulled the truck into gear and drove slowly out from the clearing where it had been parked. When they arrived at Hugh's house, the excitement of the rescue was killed by the reception from his father. His face was stern, his jaw set at a hard angle and his eyes cold and unblinking. "Thank you," he said to the deputies. His voice was clipped, closing off any further conversation. Hugh knew his father was staring down at him, but Hugh's eyes were fixed on the floor, his hands in his pockets, feet pigeon-toed from shame. His father stepped back to let Hugh in and then quickly closed the door behind him.

The silence was heavy. He knew he would be punished, marked to remember the transgression. A principle had been missed; an opportunity for correction couldn't be. He had made trouble and been returned home by the law, and that was more than enough for a reminder.

His father came into the room, the leather of his folded belt creaking in his fist.

Standing on the ice now, Hugh could still feel the ancient sting of that belt as if it were whipping him for his current mistakes, as if his father had been right. He felt it now like an ache, an association with being lost, with failure. Like back then, he hadn't done wrong by anyone. But he was punished just for being.

He looked out at the unending churn of open water and listened to the sounds of the floe. It creaked and thunked as water and chunks of ice collided. He imagined the endlessness of it and how it was all water and how eventually it would all freeze or melt and turn to vapor, like him. He'd die and his body would turn to something else, return to the earth and become a part of it, something he had nothing to do with. He'd die and he'd disappear. It was a heavy thought, heavy and cold.

It wasn't the first time he'd thought of his own death. There were so many times since Sarah was gone that he'd wished for it, hoped that maybe it would bring them back together again. But he'd been thinking about it even more recently. Especially since he'd started seeing the doctor again. He'd been stubborn about his health, mostly ignoring it. He begrudgingly went in when his cough wouldn't let up and he was forced to, when the wet, racking grip of those convulsions wouldn't stop and he'd started to pepper kerchiefs with gobs of phlegm and specks of red. He tolerated the poking and prodding, the incessant questions, the X-ray. That was when they found the cancer. He half wondered if he had cancer only because he went to the doctor. Back in the day you just hunkered down and sweated it out until the sickness broke. How would his life be different if he didn't know? He'd be blissfully ignorant, stubbornly unaware. But because he went, he had this shadow of a diagnosis, this specter of his own demise. He wondered how much better it might be to drift away silently in his sleep, unaware of why, unaware of any timeline. He would have gone about his business until he felt even more awful and then gone in to hear that he had weeks or days. Or he'd just go one night, and it would be done. But because he knew, he had the gift of tainted time. Time that he knew wouldn't last.

But if he hadn't found out, he wouldn't have tried to reconnect with his daughter. He'd wasted some time, waited a long while before finally deciding to call her. *That was yesterday* . . . he thought. What a mistake that felt like now, to wait that long. But that's what happens with perspective. Sometimes everything changes in an instant—with the words of a doctor or the crack of the ice. But he hadn't known about that when he sat at the little table in his house, the phone a heavy burden in his hand.

He'd sat a long while before finally making the call.

Clicking the screen to life, he tapped the phone icon and thumbed in her number. Tapping the green button, he lifted the device to his ear and listened to the empty ring. After five tones, the line cleared, and then he heard her voice. He knew it was a recording, but it sounded so good. It was so bright, and he marveled that her light could have come from any part of him. In a few seconds, she stopped, and the beep to start recording surprised him. He suddenly struggled to find the words he'd turned over in his mind so many times, but they never came. After a pause, he just started.

"It's me," he said. "I'm . . . I just. I'm sorry to be calling you out of the blue. I know it's been so long, and you're probably busy and all, but . . . I guess I'm calling to tell you I'm sick. I have cancer. I figured you'd want to know, or that it might be important for you to know. It . . ." He stopped, drumming his thick fingers against the wood of the table before going on. "It doesn't sound good. I'll be going in to the clinic at ten on Monday, and they're going to tell me where all it is and how long I got. It sounds like it won't be much. Much time, I mean. Anyway, give me a call."

He pulled the phone from his ear and watched the seconds count across the screen before thumbing the red End button. His house returned to the empty silence. It was filled now with a secret revealed. It was odd because no one had heard it, no one had acknowledged it, but he'd said it, and in doing so, he felt incrementally better. The tightness in his ribs and the hollow in his throat had opened some. He considered packing it all back in, holding on to that resistance, but he decided, finally, to let it be. He didn't have to. Whether she called him back or not, it wasn't solely his anymore.

CHAPTER TWELVE

The light shifted, and muted tones gave way to pastel pinks and purples that arced across the sky. It was hard not to notice the beauty of the sunset. The ice glowed. The water reflected it, and the air was clear. To the east, the deep shadow of twilight and night pulled blue black against the hum of orange that now punctuated the sky and traced each cloud from the soft background of deep tones. He looked at it and marveled. He wondered if this might be his last sunset and appreciated that at least it was here, that he was here, and that it had been beautiful.

The orange and the pastels faded, enveloped by the inkiness of the coming night. He sighed. He could have busied himself with preparations for sundown, but there was nothing much to do. He had no saw to cut ice blocks, and there was no accumulated snow to build a quinzee hut or igloo. With nothing to stop it, the snow had all blown over to the southern shore or the Apostle Islands or maybe all the way to the Upper Peninsula of Michigan. In any case, but for a thin skim of it, the snow was gone. There was just him and the ice and his pulk. In his pulk, he had materials, but they were just enough to work on a rough bivvy. He would build that when he was tired. And when he was cold, he'd drill new holes to warm up and keep himself occupied. He'd set some lines because he knew he would need to eat, and he'd rather fillet a fresh fish. The frozen one would keep for later.

He remembered he still had the peanut butter and jelly sandwich in his pocket, so he removed it, peeled back the plastic, and took unsatisfactory bites. The sandwich was dry, the peanut butter gummy in his mouth. In a short time, it was gone, but his stomach still felt empty to power him against the cold. The calories from the sandwich were but a small recharge to face the immense demands of staying warm in such bitterness. He'd seen the ice on Lake Superior do all manner of things. He'd seen it drift and still, only to be enveloped by new ice. He'd seen it crumble with his own eyes and disappear before he thought it could. And he'd seen it sail over the water like a boat, pushed on by the winds. He wondered what this meant for him. He figured it meant he had to be ready for anything, to get settled in for a long haul, but not to get too comfortable in case he had to move quickly if it crumbled.

When the light had nearly gone, the temperature dropped significantly, and he decided it was time to drill a couple more holes. He opened the sled and retrieved the auger. He walked several paces, checked his measurement, and decided the distance was fine. Normally, the holes were selected intentionally to fish a new spot of the water, but with moving ice, the location felt less important. He removed the sheath from the bit, again revealing the razor-sharp edges, and placed it on the ice. He was all business this time. When the bit was through, he pulled it out with a gush of water, walked a few more paces, and repeated the process on the second hole.

Next, he returned to the sled. From it, he removed two fishing poles, two more of the ciscos, and a twist of welding rod wrapped with tape. The latter were wound tightly around one another, with the rod curving big hoops. These were his tip-ups, handmade versions of the fancy plastic things that kids bought these days. Hugh's would raise a flag when a fish had taken the bait just like those shiny ones from the store, but his wouldn't break in the cold. Unlike the plastic manufactured ones, his were bent from wire, with hand-kinked detents and stiff springs like a game trap, so that when the trap tripped from a tug on the line, the little flag would snap up to let him know. With the tip-ups, Hugh could fish more than one hole at a time.

He knelt at the first hole and slid the cisco over the hook so that all the metal was covered before lowering it into the hole. Without a fishing rod attached to it, he spooled out the line from the little wheel on the tip-up. It was odd to him to see that line bend with the current of the water under the ice. He was so used to a stationary platform, to the line dropping straight down like a barbed plumb bob. But now it swung away from the hole, the line resting against the ice edge and bending back to Duluth. He lowered the lure until he felt it was deep enough, given the angle, and secured it. Last, he looped the line through a spring-loaded clip on the tip-up so that when there was more tension, it would pop through and release the flag. If a fish took the bait, he'd see the raised flag and then pull the line in hand over hand. With the device set, he placed it over the hole. Going to the next one, he repeated the process.

With both holes set, his mind turned toward the night. Though it was now clear, the wind was once again picking up, and it felt like it might rise into another gale. This worried him on two fronts. First, it would make for a cold, cold night. Without the clouds, the chill of space would seep into the world. It would be tremendously hard for him to stay warm. Second, the wind meant choppy seas, and he was concerned the ice might not take the beating. So far, the floe had held true, but it was only a matter of time before it would begin to crumble. That would surely be the end of him. But that was something he had no power over.

So he pushed the thought away and turned instead to checking his tip-ups once more before setting to his plan for staying warm against the cold and the wind. In the pulk, he found his sleeping bag and the tarp folded deep in the bottom. His stove could be used for some heat if he needed, but he didn't have extra fuel, and he'd have to be very careful not to give himself carbon monoxide poisoning in whatever little shelter he created or set the whole thing on fire. No, the stove would be a last resort. But he wouldn't get to that point.

He turned the tools in his mind and considered simply wrapping himself in the sleeping bag and the tarp. That would likely work, but he wanted more to hold the warmth, more insulation from the ice itself. He looked at the pulk, which formed a sort of cocoon on its own. It was close to the right shape and size to make a base. He could lie in it, be enclosed from end to end. The tarp of the pulk could help with the sides of the makeshift tent, and the tarp itself could drape over his head end, with the camp chair as a frame to keep it off his face, perhaps? He'd have to tuck it all tight in order to keep it from blowing away, folding the tarp edges under the sled, but it seemed to be a good enough plan to start. Better than sleeping under the stars anyway.

He started by removing everything from the pulk and setting each item carefully next to it. The pulk was dusty and full of bits of duff, which drifted out like hay in the wind when he turned it over and shook it. With the pulk clean, he opened the sleeping bag and draped it inside. He placed the hood near the front of the sled in what looked like a comfortable position and then draped the feet toward the other end. He'd fit in the sledge like a coffin, a ready-made tomb should the ice open up and Superior swallow him whole. He'd never surface again, but if he were ever found, maybe by one of those shipwreck hunters with their sonar and technology, he'd look like a burial at sea, wrapped and prepped and given to the waters.

There was nothing to do but try not to die tonight. So he pulled down the zipper and opened the bag to prepare it for his body.

Sarah's funeral was quiet, not because there wasn't a bubbling crowd of hundreds, not because it lacked music and eulogies and condolences, but because Hugh couldn't hear any of it. His ears were humming with the loss, and his brain was fogged in grief. His body moved of its own volition, shaking hands, sitting in the pew, standing.

Her family was religious. Religion was not something he and Sarah had brought into their own house, but they defaulted back to it on the occasions of life—Christmas, Easter, and death. Hers wasn't a big family, but Hugh's was smaller, limited to distant cousins and long-gone kin. His own mother hadn't materialized after Sarah's death. His father was there, more a cold stone than anything, present but only out of a sense of duty. Lauren was holding Hugh's hand, and Jason was sitting in the crook of his arm. The only color and sound in his memory were those two kids. Lauren was wearing a dark seafoam-green dress adorned with embroidered peonies and black patent-leather shoes with a buckled strap over the forefoot. That was her favorite dress, and her mother's favorite too. "Mommy would pick this one," Lauren had said, pulling the dress from the folds hanging in her miniature closet.

Hugh couldn't say no, let alone anything else. He just nodded through a sigh, holding back more, and managed a weak, "That'll be fine, dear."

Lauren had taken on the task of picking something out for her brother as well, and Jason wore a butter-yellow faux button-up with a pale-blue bow tie and brown slacks. He looked more like he was going to hunt for eggs and candy than attend a funeral, but it didn't matter. "This one is so cute!" Lauren had said, holding her choices high above her head. And Hugh couldn't say no. The truth was, he was numb. He couldn't make any decisions, so to have his daughter make not one but two for him was a bit of a help.

The bigger question he'd had to face was the casket. It was closed.

The funeral folks had brought it up as the arrangements were being made. Much of the planning had been squared away before Sarah passed, something her parents had done for themselves and that they'd encouraged her to do as well: to get things figured out and mostly paid for in advance. Carol Vandermeyer, the woman from the mortuary, said that Sarah's arrangements had called for an open casket, but there were some complicating factors she needed to discuss. They could get Sarah ready for it, could bring back the color and get her looking good, but there were a couple of "challenges."

"Would she have worn a hat or a veil," Ms. Vandermeyer asked, "or a head scarf? You see, there are a couple of . . . things we're trying to cover."

Hugh stared at the mortician in that cold dusty sitting room in an uncomfortable house that wasn't a house, knowing Sarah was just downstairs but a lifetime away. He stared at Ms. Vandermeyer and tried to read between the lines of her words, his mind projecting all the horrors he'd lived over and over since the crash, the images of wounds and blood and bone that he'd pushed away but that had left him both screaming and deathly silent day and night.

He blinked and looked back to Ms. Vandermeyer, who had remained an example of compassionate patience. His hands were firm in his pockets, his arms to his sides to protect against the sudden chill in his bones. He dropped his chin down near his chest.

"Please keep it closed," he said in a near whisper. "Folks won't want to see her the way she wasn't. And she wouldn't want that either."

The woman's chin raised for a slow moment, her mouth a half frown of concern. She was on the edge of saying something else, then her chin dropped down, and she blinked. "Of course," she said. "I'm so sorry for your loss. We'll take care of everything, Mr. McLaren . . ."

The service came and went as if it were a dream. A nightmare, really. Same for the interring. It was a somber gathering on a gray day in the snow at Woods Hill Cemetery, Hugh and the kids and friends and family standing around the still-steaming opening that the crew had heated in order to dig against the cold winter freeze. It was a family plot, next to her kin, and many of them were there.

Jason was too young to know what was going on or to form memories that would stick. Still, it was clear he was grieving, even if he didn't appreciate why. He would cry and cry, and sometimes, no matter how much Hugh tried, he couldn't appease him. It wasn't just that Jason was still nursing, but that the bottle could never fill the hole that was left.

Lauren, on the other hand, understood what had happened. She knew that her mommy had died, that she wouldn't be coming home. That both helped and made things worse. How was Hugh supposed to console someone when he didn't know how to deal with this kind of loss?

He didn't know. He'd never known, and it was all he could do to keep them alive until he could nudge them on to their own lives. He'd push it down. Bury it. He'd close himself off to the pain, he'd lock down so he could keep going, at least so long as to get the kids raised and on their own.

He sat down in the pulk, pulled his feet up, and loosened his boots. He thought about taking them off completely, considered pulling off his outer layer of pants too, but realized it was much too cold to remove either of them. He was about to climb into a bag as bitterly cold as the ice itself. He'd have to keep them on. Sliding his lower half into the sleeping bag, he still felt the hard, cold press against him. It made his muscles tighten and his teeth clamp hard together. Maneuvering quickly, he yanked at the zipper to seal in his meager heat before it escaped and then draped the gaiter of the sled and the tarp. He enclosed himself securely, and after minutes had passed, his legs began to warm. The cocoon of the sledge proved to be surprisingly effective, and though the storm howled outside, his body was safe and moderately comfortable inside. For his top half, he tried to drape the tarp over the camp chair, but it wouldn't fit. He adjusted the chair, half folded it, put it sideways, but no matter what, there wasn't enough fabric to hold the chair and tuck the tarp under. So he folded the chair down and stashed it next to the sled.

Back in the pulk, he pulled the tarp down so that it nearly wrapped under the sled. Awkwardly twisting and bucking, he managed to tuck the tarp under. His makeshift bivouac was complete, and he felt he'd done all he could for his shelter. The wind howled outside, but it was muffled now and didn't bite directly into him. He zipped the sleeping bag shut so that only his face stuck out, and he lay there listening to the sound of winter's fury, the ominous lapping of water, and the groan of ice. He knew sleep would come, but he wondered when, and if it would be peaceful or interrupted with the horror of cracking ice. He thought of his sledge, of how trapped he was inside it. No more trapped than he was on the ice itself, but so much more immediate. He was bound by hand and foot. If the ice opened beneath him, he thought, his ordeal would be over. He would sink into the inky depths, nothing to do but watch the darkness and breathe deeply the water. Improbable and unlikely, but he couldn't avoid it now. To survive the night, he had to nestle into that little coffin and hope the ice would hold. He tried to calm his dark, wandering thoughts. For now, he had to wait, to bide his time and see what fate the lake had in store. And with that thought of the unknown, consciousness left him, and he drifted into a frigid, still sleep.

CHAPTER THIRTEEN

Hugh heard a buzzing. Not a loud noise but an annoyance, like a fly in the corner of the room. It continued, and eventually he realized it was the microwave. *His* microwave, but at the same time, it wasn't. Just like the house was his house, but it wasn't. The colors were wrong, the angles askew. And yet he knew he was in his own home, and in front of him was his microwave.

Inside the appliance, his dinner turned around in endless circles. It was a small tray subdivided into a main, sides, and sauces. It was cheap and salty, so that was what he'd bought. The microwave beeped, and using a towel, he lifted the steaming tray out and set it on the counter. Next to it was a matching tray, its contents still frosted with cold. He placed the second into the microwave and pressed a few buttons until the device whirred to life once more. He stirred the mashed potatoes in the other tray and considered eating the food right there, standing in the kitchen. But that's not what you do when you have company.

He wasn't alone. Sitting at the round table in the alcove was his father. He slouched in his chair, an arm up on its back, the other draped across his lap. He wasn't saying anything, but Hugh could feel his gaze. When the microwave beeped again, he retrieved the second tray and stirred its potatoes. Gingerly taking the tray by the edges, he carried it over to his father's spot at the table and then returned for his own. Both trays steamed, and he sat. His father picked up his fork and turned it in his hand several times while he stared at the space between them. His gaze was intense, and Hugh couldn't quite place it—eyes blank, jaw set. He would have guessed anger because that was what he always expected.

"How long've you known?" his father asked, eyes fixed on him, unblinking.

"Um . . ." He paused, his throat suddenly dry, his voice cracking. "I've had that cough for a couple months now . . ." He turned his mouth in a half frown, as if this were an admission of some wrongdoing.

His father sighed, dropped his fork to the tray, and looked away, up toward the woven lamp fixture that dangled from the ceiling on a chain. His mouth formed a line, and he slowly shook his head. Still staring at the light, his eyes softened, then grew cold.

"And . . ." he said, seeming to have trouble finding the next words, ". . . whadothey expect?" His eyes were on him again.

"Well," Hugh said, "they don't know. Or, at least, they don't know yet. I've got all these tests. They won't know for sure until after those are done . . ." He paused and tapped his thick-knuckled fingers on the table. Seeing his knobbly joints and wrinkled skin, he was reminded that he had aged, but his father was the same as he had been when Hugh was a boy: solid and immense. Hugh shifted in his chair, pushed at his food with the spoon, and looked at the emptiness between them. "I'm pretty sure I ain't got long."

"What's that mean?" his father said, unmoving.

"I don't know," Hugh said. His shoulders sagged, and he set down his spoon before folding his hands in his lap. "I guess it means it'll be my time soon."

His father stared at him. He blinked, looked away at the wall, and then back at Hugh. "When's your next appointment? You gonna go, or just stop going and take your sentence?"

"My appointment's Monday," Hugh said. "I guess I want to know." He felt so small in his father's presence, a scared little boy again.

"Monday," his father said. He picked up his napkin from the table and wiped at his face, though he hadn't actually eaten anything yet. He leaned back against the chair and searched the room with hawk's eyes below a furrowed brow. "I guess that's your lot then. Seems fittin' you go the same as me, I guess."

The comment was a blow, and both knew it. Hugh's eyes were downcast, fixed on some unknown point, and he felt them glisten with tears. He'd tried all he could to distance himself from his father in every way, and to be taken by the same sickness seemed some cruel twist of fate. He tried to stifle the tears, to pull them back in because they weren't part of him and he wouldn't let them be. Tears had earned him bruises when he let them show.

"It wasn't up to me," Hugh said, steadying his shaky breath. "Wasn't up to either of us."

"Nope," his father said, "it sure as shit wasn't." He blinked, turned his gaze from the wall, and leaned forward to his tray of food. With his thick hand, he took up the plastic fork and stabbed a brussels sprout with a *thump* before bringing it to his mouth.

Hugh looked down at his own tray, the food suddenly cold, gray, and unappetizing.

He felt sick.

His breathing quickened and the world shifted to darkness. He gasped, breath shaky, stifled. He felt thick, heavy fabric over his face, his arms tight around him. He remembered the ice, the sleeping bag, the pulk. His hands came to his face, and he clawed at the fabric, gasping. The air was heavy with his own breath, and his lungs felt empty. His fingers searched for an opening. Behind one ear, he felt the cord of the sleeping-bag hood. Following it, he found the edge of the opening near the back of his head, the fabric pulled nearly shut against the cold. He twisted and pulled, writhed his body in the tight confines of bag and sledge. Coffins aren't made for movement. His thick-knuckled fingers forced the drawstring open. Finding air, he gasped in the frigid cold. He instantly felt better, the foreboding doom ebbing from his body with each breath.

He was still covered with the pulk tarp, but breathing was much easier, the air not as tainted with his own exhalation. The tarp shook with a stiff wind. He wondered briefly which direction it was blowing. As if it mattered. It wasn't blowing back to shore. And if it was, there was no way his sheet of ice would hold against that. Lake winds going back to Duluth didn't do it gently. The wind would whip up waves that would grind the ice into a slurry and slam it into the rocks.

No, it didn't much matter. The wind would do what it would do. And the water too. He was there to wait, to bide his time.

How long was his dad's fight? Six months? And his sickness had been caught much earlier, before the blood. He cursed the dream for reminding him of the man, cursed it for reminding him of his sealed fate. He imagined his lungs, each breath leading to the division of cancer cells. He didn't truly know how bad it was yet. Didn't truly know how much longer he had, just that his life was about to end. Or become miserable. Those seemed to be the options: end or misery. And yet, he reminded himself, it had given him the courage, or the desperation, to try to reach out again to his daughter. He laughed at the thought of calling her. Did he expect her to rush to his side? He'd hardly ever done that for her, and not since she'd become an adult. He was the estranged, hermetic old man who lived in the hillside. A sad old man whose stoicism and quiet sapped every bit of generosity and warmth.

He took in a deep breath of the cold lake air, and he felt the tickle and burn of it in his chest. It caught, and he coughed a dry, heavy hack that broke the quiet around him and peppered the fabric with a spatter of red.

The wind was still blowing, a steady, frigid pressure in the predawn dark. Above him, the stars hung in the bright tapestry of a clear winter night. Out in the openness of the lake, they were as brilliant as ever, the stars a bright white against the deep black of space. He could clearly see the familiar constellations: Orion with his belt and the Little Dipper, so small amid it all. That familiarity didn't bring comfort. They seemed to magnify the distance he was from home, to accentuate how vast the night sky was, unmoved by his fate.

He untied the lashings on the pulk and sat up, the sleeping bag still cocooned around him. The ice pack looked largely the same, such as he could see it in the dark. He was surprised that it was still as big as it was, that it wasn't breaking up more.

He scanned the horizon, but nothing stood out to him, just the stunted silhouette of distant dark shoreline, a line of ink on paper that shimmered with the distance. It was odd to be able to see it, but for that to be meaningless; it was completely out of reach.

He considered getting up and beginning the day, even though there wasn't much to begin. He decided that he should sleep more if he could. Plus, he didn't want to leave the comparative warmth of the bag and the pulk. So he slid back in and pulled at the tarp and strings until he was covered and then tied it tight with a half hitch. Secured and warm against the wind, he soon drifted back to sleep, back to dreams, to repeats and reminders of things he wished he'd done differently.

He spent the rest of the night wrapped in the pulk, and much of the next day, getting up only to walk in circles around the sledge and his gear, to walk blood back to his limbs and stare into the void of the ice and the lake. Minutes drifted into hours, and the hours melted into the day, and he was again lost in the pulk in the dark.

CHAPTER FOURTEEN

The crack shot across the ice, thudding and twanging under him. The sounds were more than enough to wake him. They were horrific, like the sound of the end of the world, but it was the feeling of the shudder and thwack of the ice underneath him that sent him into a panic. He gasped and threw his hands to the cordage, pulling to untie himself. Finally finding the string, he tugged at the free end, and the knots parted. Ripping at the strings, he opened the pulk cover and sat up. Pellets of ice blew sideways, stinging his face. The light was wan—the dim of early morning or perhaps the sun struggling against the storm, he couldn't tell. But he could see enough to know that the pack had fractured near its core. It had broken straight down the middle, and the other floe had already splintered into multiple pieces. They bobbed against one another, bumping with heavy thuds that he could feel through the ice under him. Finding that his piece had remained quite large calmed him some. But that the ice was breaking up at all was disquieting, to say the least. It was only a matter of time before his piece would break up further.

He wondered where he might be by that time and where he was at that moment. With no navigational aids and now without sky or shore to orient himself, he was simply adrift. Imagining the patterns of the ice he'd seen on maps of its winter movement, he thought maybe he'd bump up against the Apostle Islands along Wisconsin's northern shore, or perhaps he was headed north and he'd bump up against Minnesota, or even Canada, or maybe Isle Royale. Hoping for one of those scenarios was better than the thought of the ice breaking up and sending him to the bottom, or of an endless drift in the cold, but it would still be hopeless. To be out there in such empty wilderness would forgo any possibility of rescue at all.

He tried to look at the positive, to be thankful that his floe hadn't broken into tiny ice cubes. He felt the cold of the wind, the hard frozen pack underneath him, and it was as if he suddenly felt the cold of the water churning beneath him. It felt closer than before, and a fresh knot twisted in his stomach.

With his heart whomping in his chest, his adrenaline spike from the crack still coursing through him, he decided he wasn't likely to fall back asleep. He worked at the drawstring of the pulk with his clumsy fingers, the digits feeling distant in the cold. He found the zipper of the sleeping bag similarly challenging but was soon free, sliding his feet into cold boots and hoping they would warm. Standing on the ice, he could see more distinctly how small the floe had become. He perceived the water underfoot in a new way as well. When the slab had been together, it had more readily absorbed the chop, like a commercial jet cutting through the air, absorbing and deflecting the jitters of the skies, yielding a smooth and comforting ride. Now, though, it was like a small prop plane in constant motion, at the whim of the sea. He didn't like the sensation; it made him feel like he was on a boat. A boat's a fine thing, but this bob and shudder was not how ice was supposed to feel. Ice is supposed to hold, supposed to stay still underfoot. But sometimes, even on land, we can feel the undulations of the earth beneath our feet.

Hugh felt an emptiness as he stared at the sea beyond and realized he was hungry. He hadn't eaten since his peanut butter and jelly sandwich from the day before. Or was it two days? Time was starting to blur together. He needed to eat. He remembered the tip-ups he'd set before. Neither flag was raised. So he looked through his things and once again thanked himself for his heavy haul of stove and skillet. His fish from before still lay frozen on the ice next to the pulk. He thought of filleting it, its frozen body now more like wood than flesh. He had the axe and could hack it that way. It sounded gruesome and like more work than starting fresh. So, he decided to put a line in, and on the rod this time. If he caught another fish soon, he could have it filleted and in the pan before he could prepare the frozen one. If his luck failed him, he'd go to the frozen one and do the best he could. Not wanting to bet on the fickleness of a biting fish, he decided to do both.

He fumbled through his pile of things and retrieved the axe, setting it aside before gathering a rod and a lure, a big buck tail on a soft white jig. He pulled one of his pieces of now-frozen cisco meat and prepared the hook. Convinced that it would look delicious to one of the big fish wandering these deep waters—he was certainly beyond where he'd ever fished before—he found some lead and crimped the old sinkers to the line several feet above the lure. He was moving with the ice and figured something akin to a trawling setup would do fine. The sinkers would lead the lure and help drive it down as deep as he could let it go. With his tackle ready, he went over to one of the holes he'd drilled the previous day. It had iced over, tip-up and all, and his boot wouldn't go through, so he dropped his gear on the ice next to it and went to retrieve his axe.

Hefting the handle, he unclipped the mask, tossing the leather back into the pulk. From the pulk, he pulled a piece of padding that he would use to kneel on the ice. Letting the axe hang at his side, he shuffled back to the hole, his feet looking for stillness and balance with every step. He dropped the pad next to the hole and then lowered stiffly down to his knees, his axe a makeshift crutch. His knees toward the hole, he took the haft of the axe in his mittens, his posture now one of penitence, of prayer, as if pleading with the augered hole to give up one of its own so that he might be sustained. He turned the axe, and the edge reflected what light there was in a cold arc of steel. Leaning forward, he placed the edge on the thinner ice that had formed over the hole and began whacking at it. The loud thwacks shattered the quiet. Tiny shards of ice splintered away, and then the hole gave way, and the axe splashed into the water beneath. He kept chipping until the edges of the hole were even and free of snags. The tip-up free, he pulled the contraption up and reeled in the old bait. When the hook finally came up, it was empty. Something had taken the bait. Hugh huffed and set it aside. With the hole now cleared, he rose painfully and returned for the rest of his gear. He retrieved the rod, the chair, and a slotted bowl on a long handle. At the hole, he set everything down but kept the bowl in hand, dipping it into the water and spooning out the ice to clear the hole. With it clear, he set the bowl aside. The hole looked like a portal now, shimmering sides and a dark, mysterious center. He wondered if his efforts would be fruitless, wondered how many hundreds of feet deep the water was here, how flat and featureless the lake bed might be beneath him. There wasn't much point in thinking about it, but he had always been so intentional about his fishing, it was hard to let that go. It was hard not to think of the features that might draw the fish, of the currents and the water temperatures. But there wasn't anything he could do about it anyway. So, he lifted the rod and plopped the lure into the hole.

CHAPTER FIFTEEN

He was asleep in his chair when the line finally went taut.

He hadn't planned to sleep and hadn't secured the rod. It had lain across his lap like a half-read newspaper.

With the tug on the line, the rod leaped from his mitts. Eyes still shut, he reached out on reflex, hands pawing air. He snorted awake, eyes wide. He lunged, and the camp chair sprang out from under him. The rod clattered to the ice. The line curled in pigtails, then went tight. His mitts thumped down but went wide on the slick of ice. Unable to stop his fall, his arms splayed. His chest hit first, then his jaw and temple.

The hard cold was unforgiving. Bone on ice, and teeth on teeth. The side of his chest burst with heat, and his skull felt electrified. The world flashed black, then white. He felt a cold split in his chin. The ice turned dark, and for a moment he felt the warmth of blood. Tasted it too.

But he was focused on the rod, the kit skittering toward the hole like water to a drain. He launched, spread-eagled, one hand toward the hole. The tip of the rod curled over the lip of ice, then plunged into the water, the handle catapulting up. The rod clacked down, catching each eyelet on the edge. *Snap, snap, snap.* He slid to the hole like a snow angel face down across the ice. The last big eyelet popped over the lip of the hole, and his mitt splashed into the water behind it, wedging the end of the handle in place. He pressed it hard against the side of the hole and felt the rhythmic pull of a fight from the other end. Carefully, he curled his mitt around the handle, locked it tight. Despite the squish of water through the mitt, the handle felt familiar.

Finally feeling in control, he pulled at the rod. He felt a tug in response and held fast. The fish must have recognized the sudden change of direction, the resistance. Down below, its full body swung, flexing stout sides of muscle and zooming down into the darkness. It was more than Hugh had expected, more than he'd felt before. The fish's incredible strength drove it deep. Off-balance, Hugh's arm yanked into the hole up to the shoulder. His chest screamed against the hard ice, but he held firm, pinned down, the rod tugging at his submerged hand. The sound of the drag on the reel whining line out to the fish sounded foreign through the muffle of water. He slid his free arm underneath him and pushed onto an elbow. Blood dripped from his brow down the valleys of his face. Still more came from his chin. It pattered on his sleeve like rain. He coughed and spat red speckles onto the ice. His awful racking cough shook his entire body, and it was all he could do to keep hold of the rod in the water. With each breath, each spasm, he felt a sharp stab at his chest. Between coughs, he moaned. When his coughing fit was finally over, he tried to calm his chest, to calm his mind. He took slow, painful breaths, wincing.

The tugging on the rod had calmed some, and he wondered if the fish was tiring. He could scarcely feel his hand, the numbness creeping up his arm. Shifting his body, he found balance and gingerly pulled the rod, hoping the fish wouldn't plunge back down. He knew once he was up, he wouldn't have trouble with the fish, that it had gotten an advantage when he'd been asleep and off-balance. The fish was smart and had nearly gotten the better of him. But now the advantage was on his side, on the side of the rod and the reel and the hook.

Coming up to his knees, he pulled the rod and his dripping arm from the hole. He was soaked, and he wondered how quickly the howling wind would turn his wet sleeve into a cast. He would be racing against the time of freezing water and the careful reeling needed to keep the fish and not snap the line. He tried to squeeze the rod with his soaking mitt. He wondered if the message would reach his hand, cold as it was. It was more a sculpture of a hand than his own anymore, but as he told it to flex, he felt through weak signals of nerves a slight tightening and heard a wet gurgle. Drips fell to the ice. The spool continued to give line, and he turned the knob to tighten the drag. Shifting hands, he put the rod in his right and turned the crank on the reel with the clumsy palm of his left. Line pulled in, wrapping in careful circles around the spool. His face felt hot with pain, and he felt warmth running down his chin. He licked at it, dabbed at it with his sleeve. Each fresh trickle from the gash on his chin started hot but quickly froze in the wind. Dabbing at his temple, he found still more blood, and with each breath, his chest burned as if he'd leaned into a hot poker.

He kept tension on the rod to keep the hook set and reeled in as smoothly as he could. The line felt heavy, like he'd hooked a log. He imagined the fish on the other end, wondered what it was. Another lake trout, perhaps? Certainly would make sense, and they could grow to be monsters. Or maybe a salmon. Or a sturgeon? Maybe on the water, but they were rarely caught through the ice.

There was little line left on the spool, and he estimated the distance from the amount remaining. From the looks of it, about 280 feet were still played out. *She's deep*, he thought, *she'll feel it on the way up.* As the fish neared the surface, he knew, its belly would begin to bulge from the change in pressure. He kept his steady spin on the reel. The arm wasn't yet stiff, but he was beginning to feel the cold of needles through his muscles. And a thin layer of frost was crystallizing on his sleeve. If the pain of the cold went away, he knew, that's when he'd be in trouble.

The bleeding seemed to be slowing, but he was surprised how much still seeped out. Dabbing at it, his sleeve came back bright red. He'd have to see to that once the fish was up. It wasn't bleeding a lot, but it wasn't stopping either. Spooling line onto the reel and fighting against the throb of his head and the stab of his ribs, he hardly noticed the fading light of the end of day.

"You and me, fish," he said, spitting a gob of blood onto the ice. "Goddamn it, it's just you and me."

Hugh felt the heaviness at the end of the line, could sense a beast waiting, strength coiled on the other end. He imagined himself back down on the ice if the fish put its mind to the fight again. He reeled slowly, methodically, not wanting to spook the fish. Or break the line. Slow turns brought it back foot by foot, yard by yard. He cursed the biting wind and felt a shiver across his back and chest.

Damn, he thought. *Damn cold. Damn fish.*

He took his wet hand and arm from the rod and shook it, swung it in wide, straight circles to get the blood back to it. *Have to see to that soon.* He worked to open and close his hand, but it was slow to do the task. *Damn.*

He set back to the reeling with more energy now, wanting to finish it, to get the fish up. But that little extra was enough for the fish to realize that something had changed, and in an instant, the reel was whining again as the monster descended once more. Hugh reflexively pulled back, widened his stance, tried to hold. But the drag hissed. He adjusted the tension, click by click, until the reel held and he started to regain his progress. How much line had it pulled out? He wasn't sure. It didn't much matter. Whatever was out had to be brought back in. The fish kept tugging, the reel protesting with little clicks at each tug. He didn't want to clamp it down too tight and risk losing the thing with a sudden snap. He hadn't had a fight like this in years, and never out here, never in winter.

He worked the crank on the reel slowly, steadily. The rod was bent hard toward the hole. It danced with each tug from below. Turn by turn, he pulled the fish until it was close enough to the hole that he saw a glimmer of light from the deep. He still couldn't tell what it was, or how big. But it was there and it was huge.

Then the fish saw the light too. It burst down. The rod spasmed. The reel whined again, yielding more distance to the fish. Hugh cranked wildly. Line kept spinning out.

"Damn it all," he said, pulling the rod back, walking his hands along its length to the tip and then down the line. With no bend of rod and eyelet to dull the sensation, he could feel each tug. He suddenly felt so much more connected with the fish, one with it, as the two were locked in battle. With each tug, his hands jerked toward the hole.

He had to be sure not to snap the line.

Carefully, slowly, hand over hand, he brought in the fish. When it was again a glimmer at the surface, he stiffened in anticipation that the fish would dive again. It didn't. The fish had tired. It was done. Sensing the closeness of the thing now, Hugh was filled with renewed vigor. He pulled on the line and saw the bright arc of jaw, the glimmer of eyes. Its head was as big as the hole, such that Hugh wasn't sure it would even fit through the opening. But either way, he knew now what he was dealing with.

It was the biggest lake trout he'd ever seen.

CHAPTER SIXTEEN

Lauren Cox peeled back the curtains to reveal a world of white: snow caked to the window screen, snow swirling behind it, and the city and invisible lake blanketed in more snow. Despite the theoretical view from her seventh-floor room in downtown Duluth, she saw nothing but white. The curve of the lake and silver glint of the lift bridge were out there, she knew, but all of it was muffled by the thick winter storm.

She wondered if anything would even be open with the snow piled up in windswept banks throughout the city and no hint of the plows coming through to tame it back. *Do they even have snow days in Duluth?* she wondered. They hadn't when she was young. They'd all soldiered on, no matter the weather. This storm had held like this for days. *When will it break?* The drive from the hotel at the edge of downtown would be short, but in these conditions, that could still mean a long time weaving around to find the shallow spots and, potentially, digging. She'd thought enough to bring the small collapsible shovel, which sat in the trunk of her Volvo down in the hotel's ramp. Getting the vehicle started and out of the building wouldn't be a problem, but the rest worried her.

She'd come by herself, didn't want to drag her family into any drama with her father. She didn't yet know if he'd actually changed or if he was just scared. She thought back to the message, to Hugh's voice, at once familiar and still so foreign after all those years. After several of her return calls had gone unanswered, she decided she'd just head up and go with him to the oncologist. Even with Minneapolis just two and a half hours away, she'd left the night before to get north before the storm turned I-35 into a terrifying tunnel of whiteout. The storm, the drive, the hotel . . . she still didn't know exactly why she'd come, why she was letting him back in. She supposed it was because she could tell from his voicemail that his shell had cracked some. She'd heard something of her old dad in that. It had only taken three decades.

She could still remember what it had been like when her mom was around. Jason didn't have those fond memories, and his sympathy for their father was soured beyond repair. There was nothing to get back to, nothing to yearn for. At least he'd found the right direction, found leadership and role models in the air force. He worked in intelligence in the 389th Air Expeditionary Wing and had been deployed for the past eight months at the Ali Al Jahra Air Base in Kuwait.

She lifted her phone, unlocked it, and swiped over to the clock app. She tapped the world icon and found the saved time for Kuwait. It was still early in Minnesota, but he would be awake on the other side of the world. She thought of the storm, of the hour and a half before she'd be leaving for her father's, and decided to try a call. Opening her messages app, she searched for her brother. The last text conversation between them was still there. It had been months ago. She resented that it was always up to her to initiate anything with him. But still, he was her only brother, the only one she could talk to. She thumbed a short message asking for a video call, hit send, and tucked the phone in her pocket.

She tore open one of the complimentary coffee packets and placed the puck of grounds in the small maker in her room. The air soon filled with the sound and smell of warm coffee. When the machine coughed the last few drops, she poured the hot liquid into a paper cup and headed down to the lobby for a continental breakfast.

There, she found more coffee, eggs, and a bagel, which she smothered with cream cheese from an ice-chilled foil tube. Her phone was silent the entire time. No response from Jason. Through the lobby's tall windows, she saw the dull yellow glow of streetlamps, but as dawn approached, the view of blowing wind and snow simply lightened, and the gloomy pall clung to the city like a cold veil.

Her phone chimed. She set down the steaming paper cup and looked at the screen. Jason could chat in five minutes. She made her way back up to her room. A minute later, the screen on her laptop clicked to life, hiding her selfie view and replacing it with an image of her brother in his uniform camouflage, the drab surroundings of a manufactured room behind him. The image was pixelated by the thousands of miles and the slow connection. They waved and said hello.

"Where are you?" he said, leaning into the camera as if to peer around the corner. "You on a trip? That looks like a hotel room."

"Well, that's the thing," she said. "I got a call from Dad on Friday . . ." At the mention of their father, he froze, listening stoically, as if receiving orders. "It sounds like he's got cancer, and it's bad . . . And anyway, I know it's crazy, but I'm up here to go to his appointment with him."

"So everything's forgiven then?" he asked, jumping right into it. "Thirty-some years of a cold shell of a person, and all of a sudden he's your dad again?" He was upset, his jaw tight and his eyes sharp, even through the video call.

Her mouth pulled in at the side, and she looked away, hearing the same words in his voice that she'd heard in her own head so many times in the past few days. She thought back to how her father had transformed after her mother's death. Of how he'd shriveled into a wretch of a man and couldn't so much as give her a hug after the funeral. She remembered the summer he kicked her out and his lecture about how he'd coddled her. His idea of coddling was sending her with a wad of bills to get the family groceries and a bottle. She thought of the times she'd cried by herself in the living room with him right there in his chair, unmoved. She remembered the joys and the sorrows of being a kid and how she'd never shared them with him after her mother died.

But she was starting to understand that he couldn't open himself up because of how hurt he was. And it had hurt her. Now she realized that it was a survival tactic, and she finally understood.

"Look, Jason, I thought the same thing," she said. She looked back at the screen. "I wanted to ignore him, to . . . I don't know—and it sounds awful to say it—but I guess to sort of punish him for all he's done, you know?"

"Yep," he said, nodding emphatically. "That's what he deserves."

"I don't know, though," she said. "I'd just be falling to his level, right? I really thought about it. But his voice in that message . . . He was real again. I don't mean that I just heard him, I mean he sounded like Dad from when I was young." She stopped, looking to the ceiling and then back to the screen. "He's scared."

Her brother scoffed. "Well, I'm happy for you," he said. "I don't think I could ever feel that way about him." He opened his mouth but stopped himself, shook his head, and leaned back on the legs of the folding chair. He looked around the room, sighing, and then lowered the chair before looking back to the screen. "Well, that will be hard on him. He's so damn old. What do you think he's going to do?"

"I'm not sure," she said. "I think he'll end up either saying to hell with it all and giving in, or he'll fight it with everything he's got. I don't think there'll be a middle ground."

"You think he'll fight?" he said, shifting across the screen. "Do you think he's got much to fight for?" His eyebrows were raised as if to punctuate the question mark.

"What do you mean by that?" she said.

"I mean, it'd be easy enough for him to just let it take its course. Or help it along."

"Help it along?" she asked.

"He doesn't really have much to live for," he said. "I wouldn't be surprised if he just decided to end it on his own."

"Jesus, Jason," she said, spreading her forefinger and thumb hard across her brow. "He's . . . I don't think that's what he wants."

"Okay. Why's that?" he said. "What else did he say?"

"He's . . ." She paused, searching for the words, now shaking her head in her hand. "I don't know. I heard something in his voice, something . . . open, something vulnerable. I tried to call him back. He sounded different."

"He left a voicemail?" he said, focused on the screen now. "Have you actually talked to him?"

"Yeah. I mean, no," she said, shaking her head. "He called me, and I tried to call him back, but we haven't connected. It just keeps ringing through to voicemail." She suddenly flushed at the thought that he'd never returned her call. How long had it been? Three days? "Oh god, Jason, you don't think that he's gone, do you?" she said.

He huffed. "Look, I don't know one way or the other. I'm just saying that for someone like him, it might be a preferable way to go, to have some say in it," he said. He paused. "Look, I'm sure he didn't, but it's odd that he reached out and all of a sudden he's gone quiet, don't you think?"

She felt a cold rush of nausea creep along her abdomen and claw at her throat. She needed to get to his house.

"Okay, I'm heading there now," she said as she pushed her breakfast aside and began shuffling notebooks and cables around on the table. "I'm going to go see what's going on. His phone is probably just dead, right? I'll get there and probably just take him to his appointment."

"Wow," he said, "you're seriously going to get involved with this."

She stopped shuffling things and looked straight into the screen. "Yeah, I am."

"Shit," he said. "Well . . . look, you'll probably get there, and it'll all be fine. His phone'll be on the counter on silent or something stupid, and he'll be in that dumb chair with the paper."

"Either way, he's dying, Jason," she said, sounding more melodramatic than she'd meant.

He stopped and looked at the screen for several long seconds before starting again. "Yeah," he said, "I'm sorry."

He turned away from the camera, someone off-screen taking his attention. He tapped the keyboard, and his line went mute. After exchanging a few words, he unmuted himself and looked at the camera. "I'm sorry, Lauren, I have to go," he said, his voice suddenly soft. "Thanks for doing what you're doing. You're more noble than I could ever be. You'll get there and he'll be fine. But don't let him get to you. I still don't trust him. I hope you're right that he's changed, but I don't want you to be hurt by him. Keep your guard up."

"Yeah, I know," she said, "but this does seem different now. He's . . . vulnerable. And he needs us. Needs me. Anyway, I know you have to go. Thanks for thinking about me."

"Of course," he said. "Drive safe, and let me know how it goes."

"Bye."

"Bye."

He ended the call, and her screen went blank.

She sat alone in her hotel room and felt a hollowness. Her brother was right to be skeptical. They'd been hurt so many times. But her father had tried. That's something he hadn't done before.

She put her phone and computer in her bag and donned her many layers before heading down to the car park. Her Volvo started right up, and she pulled it into gear, ready to give the engine some power if she needed it.

The roads were awful as she'd expected, but much of the drifting had scoured the roadway so that she had little trouble navigating them with her SUV. There were some tracks in the snow, but it looked like most people had stayed home. *Funny how that can still happen these days*, she thought. We're all subject to the whims of weather and time.

She followed the slow curve of Superior Street as it passed the old brewhouse and the tavern and then turned up Tenth and headed through the lights. The steep climb was challenging, even for her Volvo. The drive was muffled by the snow, everything deadened in some way, numb, but her heart was beating loudly in her chest. She was nervous about what she'd find.

She finally reached his house and parked on the street in front. Though everything was muted by the thick frosting of snow, it felt instantly familiar. She felt the echoes of her memories, of the few good ones and the countless bad ones. She remembered the summer her father forced her to find work and pay rent, but she willed those memories away. She dug deeper, to the good ones, to sitting on the couch with her family, nestling into her mother's arms as her father read to them, her little brother asleep with a pacifier, bundled in his arms. How could that be the same man? She knew how. She knew how the loss of her mother had broken him. It had ruined all of them. And that brought back dark memories to her as well. She took a deep breath and shook away the thoughts, looked back to the house and the task at hand.

She hoped she'd see a shift of a window shade at the sound of her approach, that he'd be watching, would come out when he recognized her. She leaned over, peering out the passenger window. She saw no lights, no activity, no crinkled shade. It was dark.

She turned the key, and the engine quieted. She donned a cap and tightened her coat. It was silent but for the waves of wind that scraped at her car, and she steeled herself. Reluctantly, she pulled the handle and opened the door. The rush of wind and snow whistled in the opening, a frigid onslaught of wind and biting snow. She hunched against it, tucking ear to shoulder as she climbed out, arms stiff around her as she shut the door and then high-stepped through the drifts. The transition from the road to the sidewalk was gone beneath the white blanket. Finding the wooden steps of his stoop, she was careful not to misstep in the white distortion.

On the deck, she dragged open the storm door. It carved a deep, fresh arc in the thick snow, exposing three unopened issues of the *News Tribune*. "Shit," she said, bending down to look at them more closely. She wiped away snow so she could read the dates. *Saturday, Sunday, Monday.* "Shit," she said again, closing her eyes hard and pressing her gloved hand against her forehead. Images of him in the house dead, in all manner of self-demise, flashed through her mind. She squinted hard against them. "Damn it, Jason!" she said to her brother for planting such dark thoughts, and then in a clipped whisper, "Damn it, Dad." She shook her head to be rid of the images and opened her eyes. They danced with stars against the brightness of the snow.

Taking a deep breath and steeling herself, she leaned to peer in the tiny window. There was only darkness. Through a shaky breath, she leaned back, made a tight fist, and pounded the door.

CHAPTER SEVENTEEN

He looked at the screen for a beat longer, held his breath while he waited until the call ended, until the screen went blank. It took focus to keep his hands across his lap, his face devoid of the rage he felt building there. But he did. He waited until the call was gone, the window cleared, and there was nothing but the home screen and its myriad icons. This was all blurred now, his eyes focused on some distant void while his mind dug at dark memories long buried. He felt a twitch at the inside of his eye, felt the breath in his nostrils, felt it fill his chest and expand his ribs. And then he stopped. Stopped breathing and froze. He wasn't trying to. It was his subconscious pulling tape after tape from the shelves of his mind, the recesses of memory that he'd hoped to have put away forever.

Jason realized he'd frozen, recognized that part of him, that shell-shocked angry boy of his past, had taken over, and he blinked. He breathed again, felt tension from his back and through his neck. His hand came up to the screen and palmed the laptop shut with more force than he'd meant to. The other airmen in the room noticed; one jumped, the others looked away from their screens to see what had happened.

This wasn't so abnormal. Video calls were where life from back home crept in. His wouldn't have been the first divorce or birth or death that had rippled through the room and through the base. But they knew, knew that something had happened, and so did he.

A ghost had come back into his life. His father.

He wanted to throw the laptop across the room, try to embed it in the wall. Instead, Jason lifted his hand from it in a small wave, gave a curt nod as if to say he was okay. The others responded in kind and went back to their business. He pushed back from the desk and stood.

Captain Jean Simeck had been leaning against the plywood wall in the hall, staring at the ground while he finished up, and he nearly ran into her as he rounded the corner. It startled both of them, and he stepped back and apologized.

"No worries, Jason," she said. She looked him up and down. "You okay?"

"Yeah," he said, not really feeling it, but he managed a meek smile nonetheless. "I'm good. Let's go."

She looked at him, though, waiting, then took a deep breath. "Some shit at home?" she asked.

"You could say that," Jason said. Then he shook his head back and forth, looking for the words. "I don't know. Let's walk and talk."

They began down the long series of hallways that led to the Tactical Operations Center (TOC). "My sister's back in Minnesota, and she's going to see my dad," he said.

"Oh," she said, eyebrows up. "I didn't know he was still around."

"He's not," he said. "Not in any way that matters at least. He's . . . I haven't talked with him for a very long time."

She didn't speak, just waited as they made a turn down another hallway.

"I guess he's sick," he said.

"I'm sorry to hear that," she said, a look of concern on her face.

"Don't be," he said, then he took it back. "No, I mean thanks. I guess I'm just still processing it . . ." His heart was thumping in his chest.

Memories forgotten long ago threatened to resurface. He didn't want to let him back in like his sister was doing, didn't want his father to meddle with his life and upset the balance that he'd made. So, he closed himself off to it. He felt the walls he'd built around him forming again, but now of stone. He didn't want that part of him out. Didn't want any of that light in. "You know what's going on in the TOC?" he said.

She looked at him again, as if waiting to see if he'd share more or if the conversation was really done. After a beat, she nodded with a sigh. "Right," she said. "The reaper's approaching the target area, and it sounds like it's more than we thought. They've asked that we be second eyes on the feed. I can tell you more once we're there."

"Copy that," he said, and they fell into a quick walk down the hall. He was happy for the distraction, happy to stifle the demons clawing up from his past. And he hated himself for it. Hated that he didn't want to hear anything more about his father, that the fact his father was dying gave him that little bit of hope.

Like father, like son, he thought. *Goddamnit.*

After the screens had shown their grisly infrared images, the drone had left the airspace, and Jason and his partner had checked out of the TOC, he needed to clear his mind. He returned to his bunk and changed from fatigues to shorts and a T-shirt, dusty white tennis shoes, and his ball cap. He went outside, the heaviness of the heat a stark contrast to the artificial cool of the air conditioning inside. It had been 115 degrees Fahrenheit during the day, but the sun had set hours ago. It was as cool as it would get for the day now at eighty-three. Still, it was stifling. The sky was a dark emptiness, only a few stars visible over the bright glare of the base's lights, which seemed to cover every inch of the tarmac and cement.

He walked between rows of Quonset huts and found the perimeter track near the first line of fences, concertina wire bound in sparkling bundles all around the top. There were several more layers beyond this fence too, and it gave him a sense of calm and foreboding that he was both protected and needed protecting. He shook the thought off, rolled his neck and swung his arms and legs to stretch and get blood flowing. He looked at his watch, clicked a series of commands, and took off at a jog in the desert night.

After Lauren moved out, it was just Jason and his father, which didn't bode well for either of them.

Jason had been out. At a few days over eighteen, he still didn't have a license. There was little point with no car. His dad had never gotten a new one. But with a bus ticket or a walk, Jason could be anywhere in Duluth, all the way up the hill at Enger Tower or down at the lake or at a friend's house in Lakeside.

Tonight, he'd been down at the lake for the smelt run. He'd been flanked by other revelers wading in the water, catching the tiny fish. First was the smelt parade. He walked along, entranced by the spectacle of silver-costumed people on stilts and enormous fish puppets. As he listened to the jaunty tones of a rusted and dented brass band, he was flanked on one side by a sparkling reveler dressed as a man-sized fish. On the other were women near Jason's age dressed in rainbow fishnet shirts, tube tops of shimmering silver over the netting, their hair teased into impossible acrobatics.

They made their way across Canal Park, under the silhouette of the Aerial Lift Bridge and a darkening sky. There were banners and improvised drums and streaming drapes of tulle behind finger-painted effigies of the fish.

Smelt came in thick schools in April or May, and alongside a healthy group of bootstrapping homesteaders, all the eccentrics from town seemed to come out with them. Jason had started going a couple of years ago, and he loved the sheer oddity of it all, which helped him forget the emptiness of home. After the parade, they took to the cold water in waders for the harvest. Like many fellow smelters, Jason wielded a handheld net that looked like it might have been just as well suited to catching butterflies as to harvesting small baitfish. They swung the nets in wide arcs, flashlights and headlamps gathering schools of the fish. When the larger nets appeared, he took one end and helped to pull it in big swaths toward shore. Each swipe through the water gathered armloads of fish, bending the nets heavy with their flapping bounty. Jason scooped and dumped, scooped and dumped, his body tiring with the work. Soon, his bucket was a teeming swirl of the little silver torpedoes as they circled in the pool suspended at the bottom.

He'd come home with the bucket full of the little fish. It was for him. Some of them would be crisped in a frying basket, and some would go to his own bait stock. But the fish were his, well earned.

He felt a sort of weightlessness that he wanted to hold on to as long as he could. It was so different from the sullen mood of the house. In the door, he could feel the stagnation returning, but he steeled himself against it, trying to stay unnoticed. He set the bucket down next to the open door, then held it carefully to close it quietly.

The latch was almost inaudible, but his father had been waiting, and his voice cracked through the room as if amplified. "Where the hell have you been?" Hugh said. He was motionless, didn't move, didn't shift in his chair or turn his head.

Jason pressed his eyes shut, his mouth a grimace as he let out a silent sigh through his nose. "Hey, Dad," he said. He tried to make this nonchalant, but he could feel flames rising from his neck and touching his ears.

"I said, where the hell you been?" Hugh said, this time turning around to look at Jason.

Jason reeled back at the gaze but tried to hide his reaction. He didn't want to set his father off more, to launch an inquisition or whatever the hell it was that made his dad into such an asshole.

"Sorry, I was just down at the smelt run," Jason said. "I got a whole lot of them." He bent down and picked up the bucket, heavy with the water and the fish. He held it up, waiting for a reaction. He knew better than to expect praise, but he still hoped for it. He held it there for a beat, and the thing got heavy, and he lowered it back down to the rug and set it there. His father stared silently.

"You were supposed to be back an hour ago," his father said.

"I'm sorry, I guess I lost track of—" Jason said.

"No," Hugh said, interrupting him. It wasn't a yell, but it terrified Jason. "You were supposed to be back an hour ago. It doesn't matter why you're late. It's a rule and you know it, and that's it."

Jason stood, his eyes downcast. After a long beat of waiting for the next part of the lashing, he looked up to find Hugh's gaze locked on to him. When their eyes met, Hugh launched the next barrage.

"You got that?" he said, his voice rising. "It doesn't matter what in the hell you're doing, you have to communicate. You have to tell me if you're going to be late, or even close to it. It's like you think it's all just about you. It's not just you. I have to keep you safe."

"Oh, fuck you, Dad," Jason said, before realizing he'd said anything at all. He took a step toward the living room, accidently knocking over the bucket. Water and fish flooded the floor—a carpet of flailing silver. Jason stared down at it for a moment, then felt himself losing control. "You're not doing anything to keep me safe," he said, pointing his finger hard across the room in sharp jabs. "You're just here. You don't care about any of it. It's actually all about you. Your rules are there for you. You don't care about me at all. Did you even know that I'm not passing four of my classes? Huh, *Hugh*?"

Hugh was staring, his eyebrows raised, but otherwise unmoved.

"I know you said a B wasn't good enough. Well, how about a fucking F? Yeah, that's right. But not that you really care, and I don't either. But do you know how many fights I've gotten in at school?" Jason paused. "Three. I've been in three fights. In the last two months. But you don't care. You've been here making sure that I'm coming home on time and eating canned soup or frozen shit. Well, thank you for that. I can use the goddamned microwave, Dad. You're not doing anything special. I don't need to sit there and listen to your lectures or talk to a wall. I can do that anywhere."

Hugh was motionless. Jason went on.

"And it's only gotten worse since you kicked Lauren out," he said. "God, how are you such an asshole? Huh? Why did you even do that? And I don't want to hear your bullshit about lessons and life and all the things you tell yourself and all the justifications for your shitty parenting. I wish you'd been the one in that car and not Mom. It's your fault, and things would be so much better. It's your fault that she's gone."

Hugh launched out of his chair. Jason's eyes went wide in sudden horror. The chair tipped far back, then hit the floor. Hugh roared, and his fist flew up in a wide arc. It slammed into the drywall, punched a ragged hole. Dust clouded and fell. He froze there, fist still in the wall, and Jason watched as his back heaved with quick breaths. Jason wondered if this would be the breaking point. This was when he'd turn on him, come across the room, and bury that fist in his face or his gut. His dad had never hit him. He'd been short and cold and quick to anger, but now he knew his dad could use his fists, even if against a wall. Was it so different to hit his son? Jason was readying for a fight, nose flaring, stance widening and bending for strength and balance, and hands clenching into mallets of bone and muscle.

After a long beat, Hugh removed his hand, and a cascade of dust fell to the carpet. He stood there breathing, facing away from Jason, his shoulders rising and falling quickly, then slowing as he worked to control it.

"You don't know anything about what happened," Hugh said, still turned to the wall, his voice a restrained whisper. "Jason, you should go."

Jason's fists opened, and his brows furrowed in confusion. Where was he supposed to go? But yes, he should go. His father was right. This was the wrong place for him. It wasn't safe for him. Not right for him. He needed to get away from his father, needed to become a new person.

He left the smelt writhing on the floor and disappeared behind the stout door of his bedroom.

The next day, he left the house early, long before his father would be up, closing the door with that same careful deftness. The air outside was cold, the sun having yet to crest the horizon and bring with it a bit of early spring warmth.

Jason climbed the slope of Fourteenth Avenue until he reached the nearest bus stop. He knew the courthouse wouldn't be open yet, so he got on the 103 and stared blankly out the window as the bus meandered all the way across town. When they reached the last stop, the driver looked at him through the rear-view mirror, then turned to him.

"This is it, kid," he said, and Jason turned to listen. "End of the line. I'm going to be parking here for a half hour before heading back east."

"Do you mind if I just stay on?" Jason said. "I'm going to be getting off near city hall, but I just have to wait until the place is open."

The driver looked at him, his mouth turning in at one side as he considered the request. "We're supposed to clear the bus between runs," he said, "but sure, kid, you can stay this time."

Jason hadn't been expecting kindness, and it filled him with an odd sensation. He shifted in his seat and slowly nodded at the driver. "I really thank you, sir," he said.

"Not at all, son," the driver said.

That last word hit Jason. He thought of his father. He was his son, but had he ever called him that? He couldn't think of a time. He should have been a mentor, a confidant, or at least someone to throw a ball with. He was always so distant, as if he had always wanted to hit that wall and just barely held back. It filled Jason with a kind of regret. Regret at how they'd gotten to that point, at the gaps left in his childhood and his life.

The bus finally started again and when Jason eventually found himself looking out at the tall gray marble edifice of the county courthouse, he pulled the cable, and the bus chimed. It slowed at the next stop, and Jason stood in the sway and made his way to the door.

"Thanks again, man," he said to the driver.

"Not at all," the driver said. "Good luck, son."

He watched the bus leave, nodding at the driver's lingering gaze through the mirror.

Jason looked up at that heavy stone building, at the columns and the inscription. It was written in all caps and stretched the half city block of the building's facade: "The people's laws define usages, ordain rights and duties, secure public safety, defend liberty, teach reverence and obedience, and establish justice."

He looked at Duluth City Hall next to it, and the old jail just up the hill. So many turns in life that could lead to those places—the courthouse and the jail, he thought. He didn't think most who got tangled up with the law had planned to. They'd probably only realized at the very end, at the very last moment, that they were approaching something terrible.

That had been true for his mother. Thinking of her brought a different sadness. He breathed deep to push the feeling down, to rid himself of it. He closed his eyes, lifted his head to the sky until the feeling was as gone as it would be, and then let the breath go.

He turned away from the granite facade and walked down the worn sidewalk until he found the door to the armed forces recruiting office and stepped inside.

—

That was May 2001.

Before he knew it, Jason was standing in a chow hall on base, watching live as two planes crashed into the World Trade Center. And before long, he and his brothers and sisters in the Third Infantry were rolling over the Euphrates River with Bradleys and Humvees on their way to Baghdad. He was a turret gunner, standing tall in the open air as they passed buildings and people and fallen statues of a man who had done despicable things.

After six years, he finished his contract with the army and came home to put his GI Bill to use and get a degree before reenlisting in the air force. He studied Arabic and political science, and when he signed on again, it was as an intelligence officer. No longer riding in Humvees, he was mostly behind a desk, receiving and interpreting signals and human intel from operatives and assets in the field and the intercepted transmissions that their advanced electronics were able to pluck from the airwaves. He wasn't racking the action on his weapon much anymore or feeling the rush of wind and the spike of adrenaline and fear from atop the turret, but the work still invigorated him. He knew his group was making a real difference to the troops on the ground. It was because of him and the men and women alongside him that troops were coming home and terrorists weren't.

The heat was getting to him. Not just the warm night but the incredible heat coming off his body, the thick sweat. Jason took a few more steps, slowing with each until he stopped by the Quonset huts where he'd started. He was panting, pacing now, hands on hips as he worked to catch his breath. He looked at his watch and ended the workout. The timer stopped, and his stats appeared. He'd somehow doubled his daily regimen: two laps, fourteen miles. He bent over and breathed heavily, working to calm his body and his mind.

He thought of those long-ago days and the kid he was then. No, he'd left that behind; he'd rebuilt his life with the military. It gave him the structure to succeed. He knew what he needed to do. He understood his mission. He understood what it meant to have your team rely on you and to be able to rely on them. He'd learned what it was like to feel real emotions and have them tied to real situations, not tragedies locked inside your head. That's what had been so hard at home. None of it was real. None of it except his mom. That was real, and that's what had started it. Everything else was just a fabricated stress, a manufactured consequence. No, with the army and then the air force, Jason had found what he'd needed. He had an avenue to channel his rage, and a framework to manage it and put it to use.

When his father found out about his enlistment, he hadn't taken the news well, told him he was throwing his life away like Hugh's father had before him. There were no photos of Jason and Hugh at boot camp, at graduation, or at college either. Once Jason left the house, Hugh had never tried, not even once, to contact him. Even then, Jason had known it would never come, but it had been an abscess within him that took years to scar over, to fill up and harden so that he didn't feel it anymore. And yet today, he felt that wound opening anew, widening.

Now, on the tarmac in the hot desert night, he took a steadying breath, felt his ribs expand, felt the desert breeze beginning to evaporate the sweat on his skin. When he let out his breath, it was an exhalation of all that he'd remembered, the reminders of why. Letting it go. And with that, he felt those raw edges of flesh come together, sutured in his subconscious.

He closed himself off. Wouldn't let him back in. That was fine. Jason could live without his father; he'd done it for so long. What he didn't know was if he could ever manage to live *with* him again.

CHAPTER EIGHTEEN

Lauren's banging on the door went unanswered. She stopped, cupped her hands against the glass and peered in again, then leaned back to look at the other windows. The house was dark. She pounded again. Still no answer.

Reaching into her purse, she found her phone and dialed her father's number. It rang twice through the earpiece, and then she heard it from inside the house too, the silence broken by a ghost from her childhood. She could hear the ringtone like an old-fashioned mechanical bell. He'd apparently found a digital version like their phone that had hung on the wall when she was a girl. It was both grating and familiar. It instantly transported her to that morning after her mother's death. Not long after the deputy had left, when the phone began to ring. Her dad leaning at the counter, motionless, his head in his hands. The bell rang and rang. He was already gone then. What an unassuming thing, the ring of a phone—it haunted her, and for that moment, it froze her back in time. That had been the start of the end for her, and for him. She blinked hard at the memory, willing it away.

She wanted to push back, to roll back the clock to before the news that changed everything.

She looked at her screen and thumbed the end button, the ringing in the house going silent a moment later. "Shit," she said, putting the phone back in her purse.

She was sure she'd already tried it, but she turned the handle again. It turned a few millimeters and then stopped with a *thunk*. Locked.

She bit her lower lip, wondering if his spare key was still in the same spot. She knelt at the edge of the porch where the railing met the house, the snow instantly cold through her jeans. She hadn't thought she'd need snow pants for a doctor's visit. She used her gloved hand to brush the snow from the edge of the deck, hoping the motion might also wipe away the grisly images that kept playing in her mind. She tucked her glove in a pocket, slid her hand between the railings, and reached under the porch. Pawing the deck joists, she felt the cold touch of dangling metal. *There it is.* Her fingers wrapped around the key, and she lifted it from its hook.

She sighed with relief and replaced her glove, the exposed hand already red and dry from the cold, an imprint from the frozen key left white in the skin of her palm. Back at the door, she slid the key into the lock and turned the dead bolt. It clicked, and the door shifted with the sudden release. She stepped in and quickly shut the door behind her.

She had been worried that she'd step in to find the smell of death. Instead, she was greeted by a familiar mustiness, layered with the sharp tang of old age, the perpetual decline and decay. She felt at least some small sense of relief.

"Dad?" she called out, then turned her head to project her voice up the stairs. "Dad! Are you here?"

She listened for a response. It was quiet, so she started again. "Dad, I got your voicemail. I called you back but never got through. I'm here to take you to your appointment."

With her boots still on, she stepped onto the thick yellow carpet. Snowmelt from her soles squeaked as she entered the kitchen. She saw his phone on the counter, and it let out a single *ding*, a reminder that he'd missed a call.

When she looped back through the living room, she checked his chair. Also empty. She climbed up the stairs, each step creaking, until she reached the second floor. She stepped toward his bedroom, steeled herself for the shape of his body under the covers. But the bed was empty. She pursed her lips and thought of her conversation with Jason, wondered where their father might have gone and why. The unknown felt like a writhing snake in her stomach.

Back down the creaky stairs, she wrapped through the kitchen and descended to the basement. She smelled the dampness of the space, felt the moisture in the air. It smelled like earth, the stones of the foundation like the walls of a cave. Pulling the string to light the room, she found it empty too. There was one more room to check, and she made her way to the garage.

Looking at the frost-covered knob, she pulled her hand into her sleeve to insulate it and grasped the cold handle. The garage was frigid and moaned with the wind. She searched for the string on the light and pulled. With a click, the hanging bulb danced shadows across bare wood walls and shelves. There was no car, but that was expected—he'd never gotten a new one after her mother died. In the light of the bulb, Lauren imagined that old sedan that had never come back, and her mother behind the wheel, and she clicked off the light. Shook the image from her mind and focused on the task at hand. There was no sign of her father.

He was gone. *But where?*

She thought about what the house was like normally, what might be out of the ordinary, and what was missing. He didn't know she was coming, but it was still too early for him to have left for his appointment, wasn't it? He would have been sitting at the table with his coffee.

She returned to the kitchen. On the fridge was his calendar, turned to January, a photo of an old blue farmhouse above the month. She drew along the days with her finger until she found today's date. There, in a shaky hand, she saw his appointment marked, "Cancer Center - 11 am."

Her face crunched in thought, and something formed in her abdomen, a heavy thing. Jason had planted a plausible, terrifying explanation for why he was gone. She worked to convince herself that things were all right by thinking through the knowns: She couldn't find her dad. He should have been there. But he wasn't there. He was missing. *Missing,* she thought. *God, is that what I'd say? A missing person?* She thought of those horrible Friday-night documentaries that play on the worries and fears of people, about cold cases, disappearances, and deaths. She stifled the thought. He could be out getting cookies from the gas station down the street or shoveling or any manner of things. She pushed her racing thoughts aside and tried to breathe. There wasn't anything particularly the matter yet. No one was missing. He just wasn't where she'd thought he'd be.

She put her hands on her hips and stared at the floor. She chewed at the corner of her lip, her brows furrowed as she thought. She decided she should check the rooms again. She'd run through, looking for a withered old man. Now she had to go through and look for evidence, signs of what he was up to.

Starting in the kitchen, a small space, wouldn't take long. She looked at the counter. It was mostly clean, mostly empty. There was a coffee pot. It was off, and there wasn't coffee in it. She opened the lid and touched a finger to the grounds in the filter. Dry. Like a flowerpot that hadn't been watered for days. On the counter, she found crumbs and little flecks of peanut butter. The sink had more of the same, with a knife scraped nearly clean of peanut butter and bits of jelly. She checked the fridge. It was nearly empty, as usual. Nothing conspicuous there, and nothing obviously missing.

She returned up the stairs to look for clues in his bedroom. The room was gray and showed only that he'd slept in his bed and half made it before he left. Nothing more. The bed looked divided in two, the one side neat and crisp, as usual, while the blankets on the other side had been laid flat, but it remained otherwise unmade. It was as she'd known it decades ago. She knew that it had been made thousands of times since, but it looked unchanged since her mother had made it that last morning. She remembered watching as her mother's hands pressed the fabric tight from crease to crease. She imagined that now, her mother making it that last time.

She blinked away the memory and thought again of her father. It didn't help that they'd been apart for so long that she didn't know what normal was anymore, couldn't say that his favorite cap was here or there or gone. She didn't know. Still, she opened drawers and drew back curtains and closet doors. She found nothing.

She returned to the main floor, then the basement again, and then headed for the garage. Her breath puffed in great clouds in the cold space, her soles grating grit on the cement slab with each step. The shelves around her looked normal, stacked with things. There were blanks, though, spots that looked like they might have held gear. She just didn't know what was missing. She couldn't say for certain if he'd gotten equipment down to use and that was why those shelves were empty, but it felt like that to her, as if he'd been preparing, collecting. Her hands traced the empty spaces. There was a layer of dust, and looking closer, she noticed lines—traces of the taking of things. She noticed a similar pattern on the floor. It started almost directly under the light. Small scrapes in the grit. They were parallel, and maybe two feet apart. Interspersed within were tiny pale curls, like shaved white chocolate. She followed them all the way to the garage door, where they disappeared.

The pulk, she thought.

She looked at the shelves now, scanning them for that familiar silhouette of sled and tarp. It wasn't there. Walking up to the garage door, she found it unlocked. *Shit*, she thought. Her dad was never one to leave that door unlocked. *Unless he left through it.* She grabbed the rusty door handle, and the cold metal burned her hands. Stepping back, she pulled on her gloves and then pushed up on the door. The metal creaked, and it rose on its rollers and spring.

The cold rush of wind instantly filled the garage, spindrift curling around her face. She pushed the door up, and it swung the rest of the way on its own. Beyond was a drift of untouched snow that formed a sheer wall at the door. It curled from one side to the other like a wave. Her brows tightened at the sudden brightness, at the blankness of it.

Then she looked down at the edge of the door and the snow wall, where the grit tracks ended at the edge of the garage. There in the snow, like a shadow, she could just make out the compressed outline trapped in the topography of the snow. It was a curving silhouette nearly three feet wide, bright compression of white among the powdery drift. Though faint, she instantly recognized it: definitely the pulk. And that meant one thing. He'd gone out to fish.

He'd gone out onto the ice.

She felt ill. She tried to divine the timing, when he'd left and when he might return. There was no way of knowing, other than long enough for his track to be covered by several feet of drift. That could have been this morning, or it could have been days ago. Drifting snow is like the shifting sands of the Sahara, never the same, with nothing to track the time. Then she remembered the newspapers, the three issues piled at the front door.

Shit.

She paused, thinking of what to do next. He'd miss his appointment of course, but his appointment didn't matter if he was missing out there or injured or worse. Damn his fishing. She stared out the open garage door, at the swirling wind and snow, and felt the bitter cold of the outside. She imagined her father out there in it, and she lowered her head.

Lauren pulled the garage door down by the cold metal handle, and it clanged shut with a thud. Back in the dark quiet, she could hear her heartbeat. It thumped with a knowing duty, a sense of things about to change. She rooted through her purse and found her phone. She unlocked it, punched three keys, and then held the phone in her hand, staring at the numbers on the screen. She wondered if this was the right thing to do, or if she would be better off just heading south on 35. She could forget she'd ever come up here and go on her own way, her own life separate from her father. It was how she'd lived for the past three decades.

But she couldn't. She couldn't just ignore him. She wouldn't.

So she tapped the green icon and held the receiver to her ear. The line rang twice before the call clicked open, and she heard another voice on the other end.

"911?"

CHAPTER NINETEEN

The voice was distant, not only being transmitted from far away but as if they were speaking from across a field of grass, the sound deadened by the dank earth between them. A phone call can feel like the person is right there, a closeness of whispers, a presence of voice and mind. But this wasn't that at all. Oddly, it made Lauren feel even more alone.

"911?" the voice repeated. "What's your emergency?"

"Yes, hello," Lauren said. She was thrown off, suddenly struggling for words. "I'm . . . I'm at my father's—his house—and I . . . I can't find him." There was a pause, the sounds of an office in the background.

"You can't find your father?" the operator said.

"Right," she said.

"Ma'am, where are you now?" he said. She gave him the address and then his name.

"When did you last see your father?" he said.

Lauren had to think about that one. It had been four jobs, two careers, a husband, and two kids since she'd seen him. Probably not what the operator meant, but it was the truth.

"Last time I saw him was thirty-one years ago," she said.

By the time the squad car arrived, the snow had shifted, the banks drawing different curves around the house. Lauren was at the dining room table, a cup of weak coffee sitting lukewarm in front of her. The vehicle rolling up was muffled by the snow, but its shiny black unmarked sides stood out against the white.

An officer stepped out, his dark-blue patrol coat made thicker by all manner of electronics and tools strapped to his chest and belt. He introduced himself as being from the police department and asked if he could step inside. Once they were out of the blowing wind, the officer pulled a small notepad from his pocket and turned to a fresh page. Lauren walked him through what she knew, retraced her steps through the house to the kitchen, living room, bedroom, and garage. In the garage, they looked at the floor, the scraped gravel, and the wall of snow outside.

"I think," she said, taking a breath, "I think he went out on the ice."

"On the ice," he said.

"Yes," Lauren said. "On the lake."

"And you said he's . . ." He paused to glance at his notebook. "Seventy-seven years old."

"Thereabouts, yeah," she said.

"And you say his sled is missing?" the officer asked.

"Yes, his pulk, most of his fishing equipment," she said. "It's gone. Or at least, I think it's gone. Like I said, we haven't really been in touch."

"He's seventy-seven, and he might have gone fishing, walking from this house all the way down to the lake during a storm," he said.

She nodded.

The policeman nodded too, looked away, pointed his finger at the door, then the shelf, then the floor, and then stood for a minute, thinking. He shifted, looked at the concrete, the house. "We don't have much to go off of here," he said.

Her eyes went wide, eyebrows raised. "Well, that's why I called you," she said. Then she remembered her father's phone call. "I forgot to mention his voicemail," she said. "He called me a few days ago. It's what set this all off. For me, anyway. Here, let me find it." She pulled her phone from her purse and unlocked the screen, tapped around until she was in the menu of her voicemail, and she found his message.

"It's from Friday, four days ago," she said. "Seven forty-five in the evening."

She switched the phone to speaker and played the message, the two of them leaning toward the device.

After it finished, the officer paused and made a slow circle of the garage, looking at the shelves. "Okay," he said. "So that's the last time we know he was around for sure, and his phone's there on the counter . . ." He stopped and looked at his watch. "He missed that appointment anyway. We don't clearly know when he went missing, but between that and the papers and all, I think we're safely over the twenty-four hours. I'm just not sure if we should start a ground search based on where we think he was last," he said, "or jump right to the lake based on what you think he did, where you think he went."

Looking down at the grit on the floor, he scuffed his boot and made a small track of his own. The officer lifted a hand to a black block mounted to his vest and pushed a large button on the side, keying his radio's microphone with a chirp. "110 St. Louis," he said.

"110," came a calm voice.

"I'm out at that missing-person call on Fourteenth. The reporting party thinks the subject may have gone ice fishing and his gear is missing from the house. Can you get me the duty officer?" he said.

"Ten four," said the voice. "Do you have an updated location?"

"No, just the address on the call for now," he said. "Put my number as contact."

"Copy that," the voice said. "We'll put the page out."

"Copy," he said.

The officer crossed the garage back to Lauren, who had wrapped her arms around herself for warmth after realizing how cold she'd gotten in the unheated space.

"Ma'am," he said, "the cavalry will be coming soon."

Things progressed quickly. Soon an array of emergency vehicles was combing the hillside while dogs and handlers zigged and zagged through the streets and foot teams marched along paths and alleys. With the snow, there was nothing to track on the ground. With how much time had passed, there was little for the dogs to find in the air. What little they did find aligned with Lauren's conclusion that Hugh had gone down to the lake. But beyond that, there was nothing. The ice was gone. In its stead was a rough chop of frigid, endless waves.

With the transition to the water, the perspective of the search changed, and the assets shifted to boats and aircraft.

Lauren watched it all in a daze. She was the center of it. Not the subject, but the only family, the only "witness." She had to repeat the details of their estrangement so many times she began to question whether it was even real. She wondered why she'd never tried to contact him since she left. He'd never hit her, never hit Jason. Was that some line that he hadn't crossed? What's the spectrum of neglect, where one shifts from grief and acceptable dissociation to someone worth leaving behind? She thought of that now. She'd left him before. Why was she not okay with doing that now? Jason had suggested as much on their call. None of this would be happening if she hadn't listened to that voicemail and given him another chance. That had to be part of it: Deep down, she didn't want to hold that grudge any longer. And maybe part of it was that she was almost out of time no matter what she did. Her dad was dying. She didn't want him to die without the chance to clear the air. Without the chance to hear him apologize. She figured he felt the same way. She imagined that future, that absolution, and the weight it would lift from her shoulders. So, had she come for herself, then? Yes. She had—she couldn't deny that. But she'd also come for him.

She was also asked if she thought he might have had suicidal intent. She said she didn't think so, but she didn't know. She brought up the kitchen and the food prep. But she didn't know.

Despite being the center of things, Lauren had huge amounts of time to think, to retreat inward among the throng of coming and going emergency personnel.

At times, she joined the cadre planning the operation in an enormous vehicle with bump outs and antennae. Inside was a textured gray floor, a coffee machine, printers, snacks, and an array of computers mounted to the walls, each with its own mesh-backed ergonomic chair, headset, and radio. The screens had maps, comms logs, planning documents, and personnel and equipment logs. It was a hive of activity.

Not long after things had moved to the water, they'd requested information from the NOAA station just outside Duluth on Highway 53. They'd asked for the weather for the past five days down on the lake, specifically the wind patterns and any satellite imagery or webcam footage of ice pack in that area.

The weather patterns showed intense cold. The numbers were staggering. Lows of twenty-five below. On top of that, winds had been strong, fifteen to twenty-five miles per hour, with wild gusts and a tremendous shift in direction, most of it battering away from shore for the past few days. Between a pervasive snowstorm and satellite availability, there was nothing from high altitude to show where things had gone. The webcam archives did show the tremendous ice pack that had been there later in the week and, with the clearing of the storm, the emptiness of open water. What had been there was gone—cracked off and blown out into the lake. It wasn't a rosy picture for anyone stranded on the floe.

Assets were coming in from afar, though, to search from the air. A coast guard helicopter was on its way from Sault Ste. Marie, and a

Minnesota State Patrol plane fitted with advanced optics was getting spooled up for a flight up from the Twin Cities. Those provided the best hope now.

But it was scant hope—the prevailing scenario was that his ice pack had already broken up and he had drowned. It had already been so long. Whether it was the cold or the water or injury or mishap, time was of the essence because the likelihood of a positive outcome dropped with every minute and every hour. And it had already been days.

Still, they had to try.

PART III

CHAPTER TWENTY

Blood dripped from the wound with heavy plops, scattering dark clouds into the water. Hugh lowered his face to it so that his shadow erased the reflection of the pale, bright sky.

Through the hole in the ice, Hugh could see the trout.

With each breath, its gills glowed bright red against the pale flesh of the fish's belly and the white of ice. It eclipsed the hole between them. Holding his line tight with one hand, he removed the other mitt and the liner glove beneath and slid the free hand down the line to the waiting maw of the fish. He ran his hand along the bone of the jaw and found his grip just under the jawbone, careful not to slip his fingers too far in, lest they catch one of the many teeth in the fish's enormous mouth. His hand clamped tight. The fish wiggled back and forth in protest, but when he pulled up, the fish's body flexed and held still. He suddenly felt the fish's weight. It was massive.

He nearly cried at the sight of it. Not only did it surpass anything he'd ever caught, it was bigger than any trout he'd even seen in pictures. It watched him with one eye, mouth grimacing with each breath. But looking down at the fish, at how it dwarfed the hole, he wondered at its weight. It had to be over fifty pounds. That would put it into the state record category. And when he pulled at it more, he updated his estimate to somewhere near seventy-five pounds. He flushed with excitement and then shook his head, wondering at this moment. This was the catch of a lifetime. Not only that, it was the catch of a generation. This was a fish whose story would be told around barstools and campfires. Then he laughed to himself. He felt like he was being taunted. No one would ever hear it. It was a fish tale that would never be told.

He thought about letting the fish go right then, removing the hook and releasing it to the deep to swim another day. But he couldn't bring himself to do it. That seemed to break some unwritten rule. Even with catch and release, you take the fish out, look at your catch, and appreciate it. And he wasn't planning on catch and release anyway. Not with this one. No, he was awestruck, and it had to be his. This fish was destined to be a trophy, a legend.

He looked back down the hole at the gaping mouth of teeth and flesh and the thick mass of body behind it. How would he even get the fish up? Getting close to the water, he went nearly nose to nose with the fish again to look at it. He could easily see that it was too wide to fit through the hole, but he needed to try. He pulled it up, but it held firm. He pulled it again, hoping it would slide, but the bones of the fish were wedged against the sides of the hole. No, that wouldn't do. He'd need to figure out a way to make the hole bigger, to secure the fish and drill more holes without losing or damaging the fish in the process. There was no way that he'd let go and hope the hook and line would keep it. That was a sure way to lose it. He looked at the fish and at his white knuckles, his flesh going waxy in the cold. His hand was numb.

He had to move quickly.

He thought back to his supplies. He didn't have a stringer as it always reminded him of his father's. But the pulk did have line. There was cordage in the cover that he could use to secure the fish. The pulk was several feet away, though, and when he reached for it, stretched out completely, arm to arm, it was still beyond his grasp. Turning awkwardly, he got the toe of one of his mukluks over the lip. Straining, his hand still on the trout in the hole, he shimmied the sled toward him. The fish writhed, and he nearly lost hold of it. But his hand was locked by cold and clamped tighter still by stubbornness. So it held true. Come to think of it, he wasn't sure if he could release it even if he tried. *No matter*, he thought, *not important*.

With the pulk in reach of his other hand, he pulled at the cords with the mitt. It caught at the barrel lock and the knot, so he doffed that mitten too with a flick of his arm, the mitt shooting off to the end of his dummy cord, then snapping back to rest on the ice beside him. With his fingers free, he picked, one-handed, at the knot at the end. It was stuck. Reaching inside the pulk, he found the axe and removed the mask, the blade sparkling in the light. He let out a small sigh of relief and then laid the cord against the ice to give the axe a backer to hack against. Lifting the blade, he thumped it down, splitting the cord in two.

Leaving the axe in place, he pulled the free end of cord and fed it through the jaw of the fish. Passing from gill to mouth, the line snagged on the teeth. He carefully removed it, then tied a loop with a quick bowline. The fish was secure.

Holding it by the loop, he pulled the frigid hand off the fish. It was worse than he'd thought. The hand was locked in an eagle's grip, fingers unresponsive to his commands, the flesh yellow and stiff. He unzipped his coat and stuffed the hand into his parka, tucking it under his armpit. He swore at himself and then at the fish. He regretted the latter. How could he blame the fish? He should be thanking it.

The fish, now free to have some movement, slumped in the water, stunned. It swayed with the motion of the water and gradually revived. Hugh watched it move back and forth, then with a flick of its tail, the fish pulled away, and the head flashed from the hole. The cord at the edge went taut. The cinch on the pulk pulled tight. The fabric cover gathered at the grommets, and the sled slid over the hole and then thwacked to a stop as the cord found its end and arrested the motion.

Hugh stood, off-balance and stumbling. He'd been in a fight, and it had taken a toll. His body was stiff, his ribs and chin screamed with pain, and his one arm was tucked inside his coat. But he would win in the end, he told himself; he just needed time to recover before the next round.

When he felt the cold of his hand against the flesh at his armpit, though, he wondered if that was true. He squeezed the arm tight to warm it. Pacing back and forth, swearing in frustration and elation, he gradually started to feel again. It began as a distant sensation, nothing more than an awareness of the appendage. Then the real feeling came, and it burned, the aching burn of nerve pain. He doubled over with it, knowing it had to come, that having the pain was so much better than not feeling it at all. The feeling swelled, and his mouth watered, the saliva wetting the dried blood anew so that it fell to the ice in muddy-brown drops. He howled, took the hand away, stuffed it into the wet mitt, and swung it. The motion brought a fresh throbbing. His fingertips felt like they were splitting. He half expected to see blood seep from the mitten seams. He howled again, turning, shaking his head back and forth, bouncing on his feet—anything to try to send the feeling somewhere, anywhere but his hand and fingers. And the swinging helped, pushed warm blood into his hand. Before long, the ache ebbed, and his hand was hot with pain, a warm blob of flesh at the end of his arm. He told his fingers to move, and they responded, first opening, then closing. But his fingertips felt wrong. He removed the mitten to find flushed pink flesh across most of his palm and fingers, but the tips of the thumb and first two fingers were white all the way down to the last knuckle.

Damn, he thought, *frostbite.* Not much more to do about it. He had to keep warming the rest of the hand. He'd lose those fingers. He'd lose everything, he knew, but that was abstract. The fingers were real, concrete. He could feel their absence.

Damn, damn, damn! Stupid! He hit himself with the hand now, the odd sensation like that of someone else clawing at him, sending shivers across his body.

He stopped, spat rust at the ice, and took a long, shaky breath.

That'll be the fingers, he thought, and that reminded him of the old-timer he'd sat next to at the Atoll down on London Road. He'd looked like he'd come straight off the deck of an old schooner. But Hugh knew he'd worked the waters in a time long gone, probably lived now in the camps in the trees above the sea cliffs. Still, he was a man from a different time. He made Hugh feel young, and he listened to the man with the rapt attention of a schoolboy as he told of adventures working the fisheries out at Isle Royale and of the terrible winters.

He told Hugh of a time in an early-winter storm when he was working the nets over the side. They'd been unaware in time to get off the water, to haul in their catch before it was too late. Superior whipped into a frenzy. All the nets were out, and they had to bring it all in before they could run back for shore. Ice was building up along the deck and the rails, and the man had hauled in the lines and the nets, hand over hand. By the time he was done, his hands were white and stiff with cold. They'd hauled their catch, but two men had been lost over the side that day, taken by the lake. By the time they'd returned to shore, the man said, his hands were black. He told all this with a shine of memory that touched his eye. And when he raised his glass of beer to the sky and then his whiskered lips, Hugh saw the stubs of fore- and ring fingers resting limply against the glass. The middle finger was gone entirely, the glass suspended between pinkie and thumb. The old-timer took a huge gulp and then turned to Hugh, his scraggly beard and mustache covered in foam. "And that's why ye don't fight winter and the fish together."

Hugh shook his head slowly at the memory, looked at his mittened hand, and then back at the hole. It was a lesson he'd forgotten. There was no changing what was done. *And no help in losing the whole thing,* he thought. The creature just beyond him was glorious. So he put the hand back into the mitten and set to drilling another hole to free the fish.

The motions of the auger warmed him, but his lost fingers ached, felt wrong, and he swore continually at them. After opening two more holes, he had a lobed triangle that he could have pulled a canoe through. *That should do,* he thought.

Setting the auger aside, he found his shovel and cleared the extra snow that had spilled around the holes. He wanted it clear for when he pulled up the fish. Scraping the slush away, his fingers slowly grew sharp with pain from the pressure. He tossed the shovel, and it clanged against the ice like a rusty gong ringing in his ears. The pain in his fingers continued building long after the shovel was gone, and he swore, swung the hand, and held it against his side, curling it into a fist. Moments after swinging it, the sensation of the blood filling it came to him, and he swore again.

He touched the mitten to his chin and then pulled it away to look at it. There was no fresh crimson on his mitt. The blood was dry. He took a deep breath and felt a catch in his throat and coughed unexpectedly. It took hold, and he bent over, hacking painfully, his lungs burning from within. One of his ribs must have broken. Others maybe bruised. Together, they shot sharp stabs of pain when he moved wrong or let his lungs get away from him. Like now. When it had passed, he held still in a heap until he'd regained his breath. He finally opened his eyes and looked at the sleeve and the mitt, spattered red where he'd tried to hold back his breath. He licked his lips and tasted fresh copper, felt the roughness of his dried skin. He spat and then looked at the bright-red splat on the ice, at the crumple of the pulk wedged against the hole and the taut line pulling at it.

It was time to haul the monster up.

Slowly, painfully, he dropped to his knees and took hold of the line. He felt the fish at the other end like an anchor. It pulled despondently. Its fight was gone. He hauled it hand over hand slowly to keep the tension and not alarm the fish. When it appeared at the hole, he saw the jaw opening at a wild angle, the gill nearly pulling free where the cord was wrapped around it. The fish looked at him with eyes wide. With the broken jaw, it looked forlorn, defeated. It reminded him of his father's fish on the stringer when he was young, and that filled him with regret. He imagined the fish to be asking, *Why?* It was a question he couldn't answer. It only felt like his nature to finish what had been started.

He reached into the water, careful to grab the fish by the intact side of the jaw. He pulled the head clear of the hole and reached in to get hold of one of the fins. The fish did little to protest, but its weight was more than Hugh had ever felt. He found the dorsal fin and leaned back against the fish. Its bulging body slid up and out of the hole, and he wrapped a hand around to support it from the belly. Its stomach was soft and so immense it seemed to envelop his arm. Out of the water, Hugh balked at its sudden mass. The more he pulled, the heavier it became. He had to wrap his arms around it; bear-hugging it in his awkward stance was easier than trying to hold it with just his arms. He pulled and fell backward, the fish landing on top of him, the grotesque, toothy jaw flapping wildly near his face. He rolled, tossing the fish to the side. His ribs sent stabbing pains with the motion. The fish flopped onto the ice, writhed back and forth, the jaw all angles and awkwardness in a sideways grimace.

He was nearly at eye level with the thing, and it seemed to be looking straight into his eyes. After several labored breaths, Hugh broke the stare and turned away. The fish was nearly as long as he was lying out on the ice, and he couldn't help but feel at least a little bit of a kinship with it, like he was lying next to another version of himself. His chest heaved painfully, and he waited for his breathing to slow. He looked at the fish again, at its gills opening and closing, at it trying to breathe, at the wrinkles of skin at the tail where it writhed, and at how the great belly swayed when it moved.

There was no question in his mind that this was a record fish. He lay on the ice and thought of it, of the wonder of it. And then he looked back at the fish and saw its eyes. They'd gone blank. He looked at the gills, and they were motionless. He watched it, waited for the tail to thwack the ice. But it didn't. He looked back at its head, at the fish's still face, frozen in a portrait of agony.

The fish was gone, and he suddenly felt remorse. He was going to die anyway, so why should the fish have to die too? After staring at it for what felt like a long while, his gaze broke, and he looked beyond the fish, at the emptiness of the ice. He looked around him, at the endlessness, and he was reminded where he was. He was alone. No one was looking for him. The catch was meaningless, and he, too, would be dead soon. He would drift away unnoticed.

He looked back down at the fish and wondered why he had taken it, why he had let it die. What a waste. The thought filled him with a hollowness that brought him back to those fishing trips with his father and the gasping husks of those fish he'd seen as a boy.

He shrank, shoulders dropping, and he cried. It was a quiet cry at the realization that none of this mattered. After a minute, he wiped his nose with the back of his mitten and thought of his injuries, of the split chin, the ribs, and the frostbitten hand. He scoffed at the thought. He should have let the fish be. So then he did: He sat with it as if in vigil, sat in the silence of what he'd done. The fish next to him was the body of a comrade, and it was his fate to sit with it, to sit with the knowing of his role in its demise and the futility of it. It stared at him in that open gape of disbelief and sorrow. So he sat there in silence.

Then he heard it: like the buzz of listening too hard. It was like that ringing that comes from listening to silence. But it was more than that, he knew. It wasn't inside him. He'd been listening to nothing but wind for days now.

This was different.

He stilled his breathing and listened. It wasn't a boat. It wasn't a ship either. It had a deep throaty rumble. Almost a ring. Finally, in the distance, up in the gray of the sky, he saw the small silhouette.

A plane.

CHAPTER TWENTY-ONE

It was far away, a fly on the wall, but he could see the plane swooping below the clouds.

He stood, peered at the thing, and cupped his mittens around his eyes as if holding binoculars, willing himself to make out details. It looked like a small single-engine prop plane. Barely a gnat in the distance, it seemed to be floating through the sky impossibly slowly.

He watched the silhouette disappear and then reappear from behind the clouds. His heart pounded in his chest.

The plane held to its original course and then took a sharp turn and then another. It was on a grid. *No plane trying to get somewhere would ever do that,* he thought. It was a search plane. This filled him with some small flicker of hope, small and delicate as that little pilot light on the stove, but hope, nonetheless. With another turn, the plane zigzagged in wide lines near the horizon. But even with the glimmer of possibility, he felt the futility of its presence, of being so close with no good way to let them know he was here.

His mind raced as he imagined ways to signal, ways to tell this airplane where he was. He thought back to his first day on the ice, his indecision about trying to signal shore. How close he'd been then, and yet so impossibly far. Since then, it had only gotten worse. He wouldn't get another chance, he thought. This was the one time. He had to figure out how to signal them.

The plane was low in the sky, arcing like a planet around the sun. There was no way they could see him so far away, so small and dressed in grayed whites, next to a tarp and a pulk of the same hue, on ice that was quickly turning to the gray of the waves around him. He wanted to rifle through his things, to get something ready to signal, but the thought of looking away only to have the plane disappear put a hole in his stomach. It was so far away. It was a dot. What was he to it? *A midge.*

Was this the right time to light all his things on fire? The prospect of his sleeping bag and tarps a pile of crisped soot made him sick. No, the plane was too far away to risk everything on a Hail Mary signal.

His mind turned to more conservative methods. He could light the stove. It would be a tiny light. *Better than nothing perhaps?* He could spill the gas and light the gas. That would be a huge burst of flame. He'd have to time it perfectly, align it with a moment that someone from the plane was looking. That would never work. He could burn the sledge. This one was plausible but gave him pause. The sledge and the tarps were his only shelter. What if he burned his only shelter and the plane disappeared?

He had a flashlight. He could do something with that, right? The sun was muted as if in twilight, the meager light coming from everywhere and nowhere at all. How could anyone on the plane see his light? Even if it was pointing straight at them and they looked straight at it. Still, he had to try. He rifled through the sled and found the flashlight. It was heavy, and he hefted it up. He clicked the switch, his fingers clumsy in the cold. The light stayed dark. He pointed it at his face and clicked the switch off and on. It was dead. "Damnit!" he said, tossing it aside.

He thought through his equipment again, and his mind came to his fishing tackle. He imagined the flash of it, the shine of the lures. He wondered if one might work as a signal mirror. If the sun were to shine, he could flash it at the plane. He could keep shining until someone looking out the window saw him. That seemed better than burning what shelter he had on empty hopes. He scraped the box across the ice toward him and unlatched the lid. He lifted it, and the lures sparkled in the muted morning glow. In the bottom drawer to the right was the great silver spoon. It looked like a drop of mercury frozen in time, curving metal polished to perfection. The dark menace of the treble hook dangled from the end, incongruous against its beauty. He took the lure between thumb and forefinger. Turning it, he examined the back, the inside of the curve, the polished silver. He held it out with his other hand and tipped it back and forth, watching for a flash of light. The sky was so muted, the sun hidden by clouds, there was no glare for it to catch and throw. Looking at the plane, arcing so far away, he felt powerless. He had to hold on to the hope of it, though, that it might work if the light was right.

So he took the lure and held it near his cheek. He straightened his other arm, held his hand out, and made a *V* with his index and middle finger as if holding a slingshot, the lure ready to launch on imagined elastic bands. He moved his hand until the plane was centered in the middle of the notch of the *V*. Tilting the lure back and forth, up and down, he waited for a flash of light to hit the two fingers. In the dim glow, though, there was nothing. He held like this for several minutes, but when still nothing flashed across his fingers, he knew it was a hopeless endeavor, and he lowered his hands and his head.

The buzz of the plane continued, and he watched it cross the distant sky, thinking what more he could do, waiting for it to turn toward him. He went over to the pulk and peeled back the tarp. He pulled his gear out piece by piece and spread it across the ice to make it a bigger visual target. When he was done, a gear explosion lay in a twenty-five-foot circle. He imagined it from the sky, a little smudge on the gray and white. He looked at his work and felt his shoulders sag, disheartened at the passive desperateness of it, the futility. He was tired from the effort. He dragged his feet over to his chair and unfolded it, setting it on the ice. With a sigh, he lowered onto it and crossed his hands over his lap. The wind blew some still, and he pulled his hood against the cold.

He imagined the men and women in their jumpsuits and helmets, watching, looking. *Maybe they have thermal cameras*, he thought. Thoughts of warm things jumped through his mind, and he imagined his sizzling skillet. His mouth watered at the thought, and he realized he'd been in the process of trying to get his next meal. It had been quite a long time since he had eaten. And while his trophy trout was still warm next to him, he wouldn't dare commit the sacrilege of sullying it further. He still had the frozen one, though, *plan B*.

He found his camp stove, checked the seals, and began pumping air into the chamber. Opening the valve, white gas spurted out, and he closed the cover. Working from the stool, he was in a severely bent position, and his ribs protested. He shifted, reaching into his pocket for his lighter. Finding it, he flicked at the flint, even his good hand clumsy in the cold. A shower of sparks flashed into the small pool, and the stove leaped to life with a *whump*. He welcomed the small fire and cupped his hands around it, as if cradling a tiny flower. He sat like that, watching the flame dim and shrink until it was once again but a tiny pilot light in the stove. He pushed the pump a few more times and then took hold of the valve. He opened it, and the stove hissed, vapor and droplets leaping from the burner. But the flame had gone out. He reached again for the lighter, held its tip near the burner, and flicked. The shower of sparks ignited the stove, and flame burst from it in a flash. It flickered on and off, cavitating in thumps of sound and light. It gradually calmed into a whirr and a steady blue circle of flame. Convinced that it was stable, Hugh set the heavy cast-iron pan on the burner and went to find the fish.

The first fish was tucked away next to his sledge, a berm of the hole slush covering one side so that only its white belly showed. He pulled at it, and it held fast. He yanked twice, and it broke free, heavy like a wet log. He hefted it over to the stove and dropped it to the ice with a deep thud. Back near the pulk, he found his axe still on the ice. It felt light after the fish, familiar and balanced, and he gripped it near the head. He slid the fish away from the stove and turned it until it was perfectly straight, as if hanging on a cabin wall. Lowering to his knees, he squared his shoulders to the fish and wrapped his mittens tight around the handle of the axe, the bad hand painfully blind with numbness. He pointed the edge forward, then lifted the axe high above his head. Pausing for a moment, his eyes locked onto a spot just behind the fin and gill line where the meat was thick. He swung the axe down. It thudded into the fish, cut a deep dent, but didn't sever the fish. Adjusting it, he lifted the axe again and drove the blade down into the groove he'd just made.

With two more swings, he was through. It was a sloppy cut, messy, and he wished he had a saw instead. The meat was orange, and the bits of the guts visible were shades of dark rose and mud brown. He slid the fish just so to make the next cut. Repeating the process, he hacked off a ragged steak and used the axe to carve the frozen entrails from the bottom and leave a clean piece that was almost exclusively meat. He turned the piece in his hand and examined it. Finding it acceptable, he brought the steak to the skillet. The grease from before was melted and shimmering. He set the fish in, and the pan sizzled.

Now he would have to wait for frozen meat to thaw and warm. He certainly had time. He wondered if the plane still had time. He'd lost track of it while working on the fish, and he lifted his eyes to the horizon now, scanned for the foreignness of that hunk of metal suspended in the sky. Squinting, he found nothing. His throat tightened, and he was suddenly afraid. He tilted his head and closed his eyes to listen.

The water sloshed against the ice, and the stove whirred, but the buzz of the plane was gone. When he listened, he was met only by the familiar solitude of his imprisonment.

The fish was soon sizzling in the pan, though the top was still frozen. Hugh's mouth formed a thin line, and he looked at the steak warming before him, his face drooping in a frown as if the steak had kept him from signaling the plane. *No, they might have seen it,* he told himself, *might have seen the heat of it.* He felt ridiculous at the thought, the incredibility of it. How crazy he would seem if someone were watching. *A plane comes by*, he thought, *and I make dinner?*

He pushed at the fish despondently with his pliers, but it held stubbornly to the pan despite the grease. Pushing more, it finally slid to a chorus of fresh crackles. Feeling the hopelessness fill him again, he stubbornly tilted the pan, as if there were some reason to continue fighting, some purpose for which he would need calories. He let the grease pool at the bottom of the fish, and hot bubbles foamed at its edges.

Setting the pan back on the stove, he turned to the sky. The flatness was there, and then suddenly the sky was a latticework of pale-pink lace against a deep Tyrian blue of coming twilight. Hugh took a breath, staring in wonder. And in less than a minute, it was gone. He watched, waiting for it to return, but the sky had swallowed the light, and it was back to the unending gray.

Just then, the familiar whir of his stove changed. Its pitch rose from that comforting fullness to a sort of whine, as if straining, struggling to breathe. He lifted the pan and looked at the flame. It looked as it should, a blue circle kissed by orange. And then it sputtered, big golden flashes followed by darkness and then blue again. He set the pan aside to free his hands, the skillet drifted sideways, melting its own thin track as it went. He leaned into the stove and pressed his thumb to the small pump handle. The metal burned with cold as he pushed pressure back into the tank. The flame calmed to blue before sputtering again, then dwindling down to a candle flame.

And then it went out.

The dark patina of soot on the stove pulled it into shadow, and tipping it back and forth, he felt the heft of the tank. Nothing moved in the stove but the rattle of the cleaning needle dangling from a chain. A full tank had mass and would slosh and shift. This felt light. It was the lightness of sudden uselessness. He looked at it for a long moment and then threw it as far as he could. It skittered on the ice when it landed, and then plopped into the open water beyond. His eyes fixed on the spot and his mind raced. He was mad, wanted to throw everything, wanted to use the axe to hack at the ice beneath his feet. But instead, he worked to steady his breath. When he had come back to the moment, he finally looked at his half-cooked fish, resigned to the next steps.

The cooked parts of the fish crumbled, and the richness of oil dripped across his lips and chin, surprising him with a warmth he hadn't felt since breakfast days ago. He savored that feeling and the flavor.

When he reached the still-frozen parts, the meat parted in crystals, and he had to work to break it down with his teeth. It was dissatisfying and nearly tasteless but for the tang of fishiness. He worked it down as much as he could, but a glance at the remaining carcass of the fish nearly caused him to vomit it all back up. He looked away, covered his mouth with a cold sleeve and waited for the feeling to pass. He tossed the remaining steak on the ice and kicked some snow over it. It was all he could stomach.

He returned to waiting.

Seeing the plane had made him think that, just maybe, someone thought he might be out here. Those people might be looking for him. He wondered how long it might be before they found him, and after that, how they would come to get him. He imagined boats and planes and helicopters, the roar of the engines, and then the warmth of a cabin or shelter and blankets and hot drinks. The thought of it warmed him from the inside. But then the thought faded, and its absence chilled him. He shifted back and forth on his mukluks and swung his hands to convince blood to his fingers and toes. The bad hand and its dead fingers burned, but he swung it even so. He was uncomfortably cold. Everything ached. *Better than numb,* he thought, *better to feel the pain.* He looked for a comfortable position, but it was out of reach. He rearranged himself in pursuit of it nonetheless. His eyes again found that distant patch of sky where he'd last seen the aircraft.

The flat light of the blue hour shifted to a deep colorless dusk with no more sign of the plane, and his mood dimmed with the light.

Now all that hope seemed like a dream. The thought of rescue plagued him. Before, he'd been on his own. Now he was trapped in the painful passivity of waiting. He'd heard stories of hunters calling for help only to give up and wander around in an attempt to rescue themselves. He couldn't even do that. There was nowhere for him to go. He was stuck on this ice pack no matter what. The complacency ate at him, devoured his energy.

He felt colder and, in some ways, more stuck than he'd been before. It was as if seeing the plane had pulled the life force from him. Giving up suddenly made more sense.

But he didn't. He turned in, wrapped himself in that uncomfortable shroud, and prepared for another long, cold, dark night.

CHAPTER TWENTY-TWO

After the first couple of days, the aircraft had found nothing.

Lauren was at the command center again.

She sat at a stout table that was bolted to the floor, getting briefed on the status of the search. Across from her sat Mark Calvin, a uniformed man in his late sixties who was running his hands through his curl of gray hair. In his hand was a pen, which he used to jot notes on a legal pad that sat alternately in front of him on the table or in his lap. At the corners of the room were more uniformed folks, arms crossed, listening patiently.

"Ms. Cox, I'm not going to sugarcoat this," Calvin said. "This is not an easy search, and we're not making the progress we want. That's also not a surprise, given the situation. We're working as hard as we can, and we're doing our best to continue to gather more information on how to find your father."

She nodded silently, waiting for him to continue.

"After our initial search seemed to confirm the theory that the lake was his destination, we came back to the table to run what we call a

POCSA," he said. "That stands for Probability of Containment Scenario Analysis. It's basically a bunch of crazy equations. We gather all of our data, and we gather all of the minds working on this to come up with what we each individually think to be the most likely scenario, the most likely way we think things have gone, how he might have responded, and where we think he might be."

Calvin set the pen down and leaned forward. "Look, I know it probably sounds kind of like reading tea leaves, but trust me, this is good science supported by good data, and this is one of the best tools in our toolbox for concluding an ongoing search," he said. "This is how the navy found and sank U-boats in World War Two, and it's how we've found a lot of missing folks.

"Our POCSA results continue to point to the lake. So, we've got our air assets running search patterns over the water based on the most prominent wind and current scenarios," he said. "There's the drift of the ice and all that, but it's much more complicated because of how much it's broken up. It's a huge patchwork out there. It makes for a hell of a visual field to pick something out from. The thermals should help, but we have to be looking at him in order to see him, and the search area spreads further with every hour. It's breaking up, and the ice is spreading as we speak."

"Okay," Lauren said. "I guess I'm not sure what you need from me."

"Sure," he said, his pen finding a line. He jotted down a quick note. "Look, a big part of this is the weather, right? How much do you think he'd hold on?" he said. Then he winced, leaned back, and scratched at an imagined itch at the back of his head. "No, let me rephrase that. A big part of his survival out there is how well he'd be able to manage the cold, to build a shelter or figure out how to stay warm. Do you think he'd be equipped for that?"

"I see what you're asking," she said. "He's a stubborn old bastard, and he's been out in weather colder than this for sure. I don't know, I think he'd be able to stick it out."

He nodded. "All right, well, we'll keep doing what we can, and we'll keep you updated as we have anything to share."

He stood, shook Lauren's hand, and showed her to the door.

She left down the steel mesh steps and drove up the hill back to the house.

She hadn't been told to leave things as they were, so she'd taken to exploring some of the mementos. The living room was the same cold, bare space she'd known. It hadn't changed since that day she realized she was on her own. She wandered upstairs to his bedroom, the room that he used to share with her mom.

On the dresser were pictures of her mom and the two of them together, faded memories of riding the tubes at the ski hill on the other end of town, of holding a stringer full of fish on a green summer day, of a warm day on a rocky beach. The images pulled at something deep within Lauren.

Her phone buzzed with a dull vibration in her purse, and she set the photos down. She didn't recognize the number, but it was a 218 area code, so she picked it up.

"Ms. Cox?" the voice said.

"Yes," she said.

"Ms. Cox, it's Mark Calvin from the county," he said. "Our search birds are getting called away. The coast guard bird was called back to their home base, and there's another call out in the sticks that *Trooper 9*, the state patrol bird, is headed for to get eyes on a couple of kids. We'll pick the grids back up when we're able to get them back here."

"Oh," Lauren said. She was surprised. There was so much more to do, and it seemed so abrupt. They'd just been planning the next steps. "Are you calling off the search?"

"No, ma'am, we're just pausing that aspect of it right now," Calvin said. "We're working to get other assets in the air, and we'll call these back as soon as we can. We have a request in with the RCMP to see if they can run grids further north. I'm hopeful one of their C-130s can run some big swaths in the lake. Until then, and until we hear from them, you'll just have to sit tight. I'm sorry, that's probably not what you want to hear."

"It's not, but thank you for letting me know," she said. "And thank you for everything you and your team are doing."

They ended the call, and she sat down on the edge of the bed. She felt deflated, empty, but what more could she do? What more could any of them do?

CHAPTER TWENTY-THREE

Eventually, his world of endless shadow was interrupted by a dim sliver of pinks and purples at the horizon. The direction confused him. He'd expected it from the other side of the ice. But there it was, the coming light of day. It had risen in the east, as always, and he turned his mind to it, to truth and reality.

This new light seemed to color the air itself, as if it were almost liquid, like he was inside a blossoming bruise, pale flesh tingling with the shades of a coming ache.

The air was bitingly cold, much colder than the water of Lake Superior beneath him, colder, it seemed, than the previous days. All around his little island of ice, the lake steamed with plumes of sea smoke. It curled at the water, conjuring at the surface as if a fragile inception of a thought that might simply disappear in the breath of the lake. Somehow, inches above the water, it coalesced into a mere idea of steam, something that might actually happen if it were allowed to. Still, he imagined it disappearing, felt the fragility of it. But it didn't. It grew, forming a column that rose, heavy and thick. And it kept rising, for hundreds of feet, each column combining into a wall of dancing gray, surrounding him and his small island of ice so that he felt he was in the eye of a hurricane.

Then, he saw a figure in the distance.

It was a man, walking through the curtains of steam in that early-morning light, appearing like a phantom from the empty beyond. The form moved through the smoke, tendrils of haze curling around a familiar gait. Shoulders hulked under a blue work shirt, breast pocket still filled with a pack of cigarettes. His pants formed columns of the same color, and it was as if he had come directly from the foundry. Everything about him was so familiar, and it stirred in Hugh a mixture of both longing and fear.

It was his father.

As a child, Hugh had longed to be seen by his father, to be embraced by him, accepted by him. But he knew better. Knew better then and knew better now, to expect the cold and distant at best, and the belt at worst. So Hugh steeled himself, lifted his back, widened his stance, and firmly crossed his arms.

The figure approached. It was the slow lope he knew, a steady, methodical step that barely moved from left to right, as if avoiding any expenditure of effort beyond the necessary. As he approached, Hugh heard the wafting sounds of footfalls on ice. His chest tightened and the flurry of emotions he'd experienced as a boy washed over him anew, the trepidation of retribution and punishment and that insidious yearning for approval.

His father closed to fifteen feet, then ten, then the last steps until he stopped so close that the two could have embraced, if they ever did that. Instead, he put his hands in his pockets.

Hugh waited for him to speak.

His father looked just as he remembered him. He'd only been sixty-five, but his hard life seemed to add ten or twenty years, his deep wrinkles more a sign of chronic toil and strain than of old age itself. He looked Hugh up and down, looked at the rope of the pulk in his hand and then at the bulk of the thing before surveying the ice and the fish and the lake beyond. His mouth was open in an uncomfortable grimace, and he closed it now, his lips squeezing to the side as if a thought had crossed his mind that he knew better not to say. Instead, he sighed, his shoulders rising slowly before a quick drop.

His eyes circled the ice, took in the heap of gear spread across the ice, and lingered on the enormous fish before landing back on Hugh's slumped form. "That's quite the fish," he said. "Shame though, really." He paused, looked at Hugh's arm. He pointed a finger to it. "You'll lose that now, you know?" Hugh looked down, moved the limb clumsily, and nodded.

"This is a hell of a spot you've got yourself into," his father said. "I expect it ain't what you were going for. I'd gamble you hadn't'a thought of the consequences much, and now you're thinking to yourself: *What in the hell have I gotten myself into?*

"I expect there's a lot of that," his father said, "a lot of regret." He stopped and stared into the distance. He looked on, and they held in that quiet for a long while, a conversation in puffs of steam and nothing more.

It was then that Hugh realized his father wasn't dressed for the weather. That was both odd and made sense to him. He didn't look cold; he was just there. Hugh considered offering the tarp or the sleeping bag for him to wrap himself in, but it wasn't his place to offer anything to his father. That would only result in a slap across the ear and a reprimand that he'd get his own damn blanket if he needed it. He was just a boy; he didn't know what his father needed, and it was an insult to pretend like he did.

"Ya know," his father said, still staring off into the distance, "if there's one thing I gave you, it was regret. So I can't much blame you for feeling it yourself. I can't much blame you for a lot of things, and that's sure as shit one of 'em. That one's on me. But I can tell you that whatever pile of it you got in your gut, it ain't nothing compared to the shit ton I've got in my belly."

He stopped and looked at Hugh. "Regret, I mean," he said. "Things I wish I'd done different."

Hugh shifted uncomfortably. This was more open than his father had ever been. He didn't know what to do about it, or worse, what to expect next. There was something to knowing that a conversation would end with a lashing and being prepared for it. But the unknown now buzzed around him like a cloud of mosquitoes.

"I guess what I'm trying to say is . . ." His father paused to find the words as his hands joined over his large belly, thumbs drawing nervous circles around one another. "I'm trying to say I did a shit job. I did wrong and a shit job and I wasn't man enough to admit it. I wasn't man enough to tell you how hard it was. I thought I had to be the one that never broke, and that nothing could hit me. And that made me an asshole. That made me . . . It made me think . . ." He turned away again, stuffed his hands in his pockets, and searched the column of smoke.

"I thought I had to be tough, to show I was tough and to show you I was tough," he said, looking back at Hugh. His father's eyes were glassy. "The truth of it is, truth of it was, that I was broken. I still am. I'm a broken fool of a man who thought he had to be tough on his kids in order to be strong and had to be tough on everyone to show how much of a man he was. But I was a piece of shit, and I treated you like one too. Goddamn, I was a fool. I didn't know it, but I know it now. I was a piece-of-shit fool. And all those years of acting like I was better than everyone, and what did it get me? Nothing and no one.

"Aw hell. Why am I saying all this? Why am I bothering you out here?" he said, looking around him. "This is my goddamn fault. It's my goddamn fault you're out here. This . . ." He took his hands from his pockets to gesture at the emptiness. Hugh watched his thick, ruddy hands as they circled, exposed to the cold. "This, and your perdic'ment here is my fault. It's my fault you're still alone now, is how I see it. I taught you to be alone and to not trust nobody, and what did it get you? What did it get me? Nothing."

He was about to go on, but Hugh interrupted him.

"Nothing?" he said, his voice scratchy after so much silence. "Nothing is what it *would* have gotten me. But I forgot you, and all your shit."

Hugh's face was hot now, in spite of the cold wind. "I put you behind me, got rid of you," he said, pointing the ruined hand at his father. "But then, when it all came apart, I had nothing to fall back on. Didn't know how to cope. It's because of you that I didn't know what to do at all and turned back into a goddamn husk of a man after Sarah was gone." He paused, his voice breaking as he said her name. He looked away and shook his head and then, as much to the ice as to anyone, he said, "It would have been better if you hadn't been there."

His father's face was downcast, and he nodded slowly. "That's fair," he said. "That's all fair and true. And I didn't come here to argue with you about that because you're right. I guess . . ." His father put his hands back in his pockets. "I guess . . . what I'm trying to say is . . ." He shook his head slowly as if trying to decide if he would say the words in his mind or shove them back down into the cold below. "I guess what I'm sayin' is that I'm sorry."

His shoulders dropped, and his chin fell to his chest. "I'm sorry for how lousy I was to you. And I'm sorry for not telling you sooner." He paused and toed the snow with his shoe. "I'm sorry for not telling you that I loved you, and for being so weak as to treat you the way I done."

His head shook slowly side to side, and his jaw tensed into a thick frown. It was an expression Hugh had never seen, and when he squeezed it tight, tears fell onto the snow. Those, he'd truly never seen before.

"Anyway, I wanted you to know that," his father said. He stopped, bobbed his head a few more times, and shook it side to side.

Hugh didn't know what to say. He was speechless, and for a moment, the cold of the lake and the icy air were gone. He looked across the short distance to his father, who stood there, looking at him now from under the bridge of his furrowed brow.

Hugh looked away at the emptiness around them, at the whisper of crimson that was the coming light of dawn and then at his muklukked feet. He felt a sort of release, and a tightness in his throat and back that he hadn't realized was even there relaxed, and he sighed. He met his father's eyes, his mouth closed to a thin line, and he slowly nodded.

His father's chin dropped to his chest. "Okay, then," he said. "Well, anyway, I'll leave you now."

He turned to walk away, but after just two steps, he stopped, half turning back to look at Hugh.

"One more thing," his father said. "You're a stronger, better man than I ever was. I want you to know that." He held Hugh's gaze for a moment but didn't wait for an acknowledgment or a response this time. He just turned and kept on, walking away toward the edge of the ice and into the mist.

Hugh stood for a long while, his breath puffing clouds in the cold. The columns of sea smoke shifted from the pale lavender of predawn and glowed with the amber of the rising sun and then turned to gray as they climbed above the horizon. He felt the slow grip of cold on his feet and hands, the emptiness of the bad one, and he introduced a slow motion to his limbs, a bending and straightening of arms and legs, opening and closing of hands such as he could, and the bend and twist of his ankles. The empty feeling slowly ebbed, and the burning returned. After doing this until he could no longer remember when he'd started, he was as warm as he would get in his cocoons of insulation. He slowed the motion and studied the dancing steam around him. The rest of the world was stillness. It was cold, and the waves were gone, like the ice was adrift on smoke-veiled glass. There was nothing, and he was alone. He imagined the vastness around him, this expanse of openness. It bent around him, beyond the horizon to more water and, eventually, distant shores.

He thought of his time at home, his children, their mother, his mother, and his father. They were all gone, far away or dead. He was as much alone at home as he was on the ice. It felt different, but why? It was really the same thing, to be alone out here, as it was to be alone in that empty house. There was no one at either place. This was, in some ways, more calming. It didn't have the pall of what once was. It only had the inevitable shadow of what was to come: water, only water. There'd be nothing to remain of him but the husk of his body in the deep. At least he knew.

Unless, of course, he drifted into some purgatory. He imagined falling asleep, awakening on this same raft in the afterlife. That thought chilled him as much as the air around him and the ice under him. How would he know? That, he thought, would never end: his own hell. *No fire and brimstone, but perhaps more fitting to freeze.*

Despite the apprehension, he felt the cold of the morning biting through his layers. Soon he would need to shelter. He would climb into his pulk bivouac again to protect himself from the storm.

He was biding his time on a much shorter clock now, didn't have to think about the months or years it would take for the sickness to claim him, the act of going on for the sake of it. He was just waiting. The fear had left him now, and he felt more apathy than anything, a sort of calm. That was fucked up. How could he be calm? He was dying a slow, frigid death from exposure and the eventual crumbling of his raft of ice. How could he be calm? He imagined the pain of not knowing. The remnants of his family would not truly know, and that pained him. *And they wouldn't care, would they?* he thought. But he would know. He wasn't the one waiting for news. He was the one waiting for the end. He would see it, and it would envelop him. There was no question, would be no question for him. It would be final.

CHAPTER TWENTY-FOUR

It wasn't a long drive, maybe half an hour, maybe more with the dark and the snow. A drive through the hillside, up Sixth to Rice Lake Road, and then that winding drive up past the apartments and the school, following the jog along Arrowhead, then catching Rice again up beyond the airport. Past that was mostly open country, a few repair shops, a country bar at Martin Road, a couple turns, and then the marshlands beyond. There were no lights up there, except for at the Little Minnow country bar and gas station, and that little town hall miles farther. It was like crossing into space once you were up there. She'd keep going, all the way to Island Lake.

All the way to the ice road.

There wasn't much official about it, no flags or signs or markers, just a slope down at the boat launch where dirty tire tracks from the road turned into dirty tracks on the ice. It wasn't like the roads on Vermilion or Shagawa, which were maintained. Here it was just another way to get across the lake. It was a shortcut to her friend's house on the far side, a way to avoid the long, winding country roads that wove around the reservoirs, and it let her drive under the open sky and the blanket of stars.

She'd been on it countless times. Tires ground through grit on the landing and then, seamlessly, found purchase on the ice.

You could have been forgiven for forgetting you were on a lake. It was so smooth and normal once you were out there. As natural as could be. The hardest part was putting tires on the ice. There was something unnatural about it. There was this big body of water most of the year, a huge flat disk of swaying surface and secret depths. To go from that to a solid surface was a kind of alchemy, and when you took the car to it, it felt a bit like blind faith. But as with faith, once you gave yourself over to it, once you put the tires on the ice, it was oddly freeing, as if an entire world was suddenly open to you.

She followed the tracks of cars before her, heading northeast into the dark yin-yang of white lake ice and black night sky. She cranked up the fan and the heater. Outside, it was cold. The wind was harsh. It had been maybe five degrees when the sun dipped below the horizon a few hours before. It was colder now, but that was typical for early January in Duluth. The night was dark and clear, a sliver of moon just rising from behind the earth.

Getting out was no longer normal, and she relished the quiet and the solitude in anticipation of the upcoming social gathering. There would be warmth and conversation, wine and fruit, champagne and pie. How wonderful to feel like an adult and an individual person again. And still, she felt that guilt of being away from them. She glanced down at the dash of her car, at the little photos flittering on the vents—pictures of Lauren and Jason laughing together in diapers, of the family at the start of the Mississippi River in Itasca State Park, and of her and Hugh together, laughing at the beach. They danced in the warm air, and they warmed her from the inside now too. How good to be away and to then return. She let her eyes linger on those happy memories and thought of the scene she'd just left, of her husband and kids still in their warm living room and her daughter's arms tight around her, her face buried in Sarah's neck, as if searching for every possible inch of contact. Those hugs were what she lived for. The embrace had both filled Sarah and made her question her plans to leave in the first place. She felt it deep in her core, this feeling of home. That she should stay. But she'd committed. She had been on her way out the door. She was strong—loving and strong—and to say goodbye is sometimes the most important thing to do. The hardest thing to do.

How strange to want so desperately for a break and then to think so much of him and the kids when she finally got one. The irony of it. She took a breath and reminded herself that she'd been planning this night for a long time. It wasn't her time to step in and tidy things up. Hugh had it. The two were a team. They complemented each other. She knew he had things under control.

She smiled at the thought, at the image of her family, and focused again on the icy road.

The darkness of the shoreline moved in the background, bays coming and going like the fingers of wraiths. And then a shadow passed in front of her. Like an arm reaching out from that dark beyond, it swept toward her. The pale of ice was replaced by the dark of sky.

It was too quick for her to react. She only recognized it, felt the tensing of things. Widening eyes, throat heavy, pressure in the chest. And then it was there.

She was between worlds. Like a plane taking flight, the hum and vibration of tires disappeared. But there was no sense of lift. It was heaviness. A momentary release. For an instant, she was suspended in freefall. Outside rushed past. Headlights pleaded. But there was only darkness—the blanket of sky, and that empty shadow where there once was ice. The engine whined.

Then a sudden stop. Headlights buried down and a curtain of brown water shot up. The seat belt cut at her shoulder and lap. The bottle of champagne rocketed forward from its rest on the back seat. It shattered on the dashboard, the foil-wrapped neck punching through the windshield. Her body met the sudden hardness of the steering wheel at her ribs, and it cracked her forehead.

Her vision narrowed in throbs. The car slid, then the back tires and trunk slumped through the last of the thin ice. There was a sensation of floating, and she felt the vehicle drift sideways, spinning around the sinking engine compartment. The wash of headlights dimmed beneath the surface. Steam hissed and popped from the hood, then the motor shrieked to a stop. Water climbed up the cab. It filled the footwell and climbed her legs. It was unimaginably cold. The world was tilting, listing.

Moving slowly, blood dripping hot now from her forehead, she pushed back from the wheel against the downward tilt of the car as the heavy engine pulled it into the lake. Her hands found the strap of her seat belt, and then the buckle, now underwater. Her thumb found the release, but when she pushed, nothing happened. She pushed again. Nothing. Water found her stomach. She gasped with the sudden cold. It groped at her chest.

Then water gushed from the vents. The photos of her family peeled from the dash and floated around her.

Outside, dark water climbed over the wipers and up the windshield. When it reached the hole from the bottle, it rushed into the car. Darkness was above, the water shimmering brown below.

With another press of the release, her seat belt finally came free. The water was at her neck. Her body gasped in spasms. She tried to breathe deeply, to catch the last bit of air before the car was filled. And then there was no more. She was in the inky freeze of the lake, the sound of the catastrophe instantly muffled in liquid. Her hands pawed the window, found the upholstery below and the handle. She tried it, but the door wouldn't open.

The headlights flickered, alternately illuminating her murky demise and dooming her to blackness. She felt across the door and found the crank for the window, turning it first in the wrong direction. She found the right one, the glass lowered, and her ears popped. She tried the door once more. Nothing. The lights flickered, then finally went black for the last time.

Her lungs burned now; her neck felt thin. Finding the window crank again, she turned it wildly. The opening grew until the crank found its stop. Placing a hand on each side, she pulled through and pushed off from the car. Her chest spasmed for air. The sinking car threatened to pull her down, and she kicked away. With every inch, the pull of the car lessened.

The world was black. But at the surface, she made out the pale glow of ice, lit by the sliver of moonlight. And among that glow was the dark shadow of the hole. It looked small from where she was, and she kicked toward it with everything she had. One shoe came off, and then the other.

Air. It was all she could think about. Her chest bucked, and she clenched her jaw tight, groaning at the effort and the pain. When her head finally broke the surface, she gasped, a sort of shrieking scream. And she took huge breaths. *Air.*

Then she felt the wind. It was horrible, cold needles pelting her skin, instantly turning her wet hair solid. She began to shiver. She felt her muscles beginning to cramp. She pulled toward the nearest edge of the hole. Bubbles came to the surface around her.

At the ice, she pawed at the sharp edge, pulled at it, only for it to break free. Her jaw chattered, and she felt her breath gasping again. Finally, when she pulled at the ice, it held. Her hands, bloodied now, left streaking prints. She pulled but couldn't get up. Kicking and pulling, she managed to get her torso out of the water. The wind ravaged her all the more. Nevertheless, she pulled out from the water until her body was on the ice. On instinct, she curled up into a ball.

It was so cold. She knew it was too cold.

No, she thought. *No, I can't go. This can't be it.* She thought of those photos drifting somewhere below, of her son and daughter. Of how she'd never see them again. Of how they would grow up without a mother. Of how she'd failed them. The thoughts clawed at her insides like a rake.

But her mind was slipping too.

And soon, all she knew was calm and dark.

CHAPTER TWENTY-FIVE

Hugh thought of that Tuesday. He ached for what they'd had before. He wished she could be here, could tell him it would be okay. Soon he might be with her again, and he felt like maybe he could be that man again.

But that opened a crack in his hard shell, and it let in the cold wind. It burned at his skin like icy water on raw nerves. His chest heaved at the memory, and the cold of the chilled lake air burned him from the inside, catching at his throat. His lip shook, and he felt his eyes well with tears. They instantly formed a rime of ice, and he wiped at them with the back of his mittens in an attempt to keep them from cementing his eyes shut.

His hope was gone, his armor of stoicism was broken, and he fell to his knees. His face turned down, chin to chest, and the tears fell from his closed eyes in heavy drops.

He felt the weight of solitude now, of how long he'd been without her. It pressed across his chest as if he were trying to breathe at the bottom of the lake, ribs aching with the effort, stomach burning with knots.

He didn't move. His mitted hands hung at his eyes. He felt a tugging at his neck, a frown that went down to his chest and pulled at his heart. Such a mundane moment. He'd thought there'd be a lifetime of those, that she might always be there. What he would have changed knowing that wasn't true. How could he have known then? He couldn't. And from then on, he'd felt only regret. How he would have stepped close to her, felt the curve of her back, the warmth of her skin, smelled the sweetness of her hair.

But he hadn't known.

He looked down at the inky cold of Lake Superior, at the short inches of ice between him and that endless water. He could feel that ice edge in his core, as real as if it were a knife in his belly. It was cold, penetrating. It seemed to pull him, and if he stepped too close, a blue-pale arm might reach out and yank him in.

He imagined stepping off the edge into the water. It would be a horrible few minutes of stabbing cold and gasping sudden indecision. And then the calm of the cold would overtake him, and he could slip under and it would all be over. How soothing that might be, to end all this nonsense and worry, and maybe to find Sarah somewhere in that great beyond.

It was tempting.

But that wasn't better, was it? It didn't feel like it to him, didn't feel like the solution. Felt like it would leave something undone. *That would be quitting*, he thought, and he wouldn't quit. He was too stubborn.

So he went back to his sort of ritual, a repetition: look up, look down, side to side.

Nothing. No change. Hugh's feet crunched the snow on the ice, and he remembered the silhouette of that plane, willed it to return. He would be able to see it now by the sparkle of its lights. But there was only sky.

He stepped back, his mukluks in stark contrast against the white of snow on ice, and felt the heaviness of knowing how close he was to his wife. Or to her fate. It was a dark connection, and rather than offering the prospect of a meeting, it felt like a leap into the dark cold of the lake would usher in a shared emptiness, both of them doomed to a shadowy silence. Instead of being reunited, they would be locked away in separate cells, forever just out of reach.

He felt his wife there, waiting. She sat in a dimly lit grotto, a cave, or a cell. Hands wrapped around knees, she stared into an unknown distance. He watched her in silence, and she sat in the same. That stillness was part of this new existence. She had never been that way in life. Never still or silent. But that is what happens over time without stimulation. That is what happens when you are subjected to the emptiness of isolation. Time stills. Slows. A nothing room echoes your thoughts until they have played out and there is nothing left to echo. And then there is nothing.

I'm in it too, now, he thought, *the same fate.*

Even so, he recognized that her world was not reachable from his.

He'd tried.

He'd spent countless hours pleading and speaking and yelling and crying, only to have her silence in return. She never spoke to him. She couldn't hear him. No matter how much he pounded on the walls of that cell, she sat in silence, slowly breathing in a world without time, features, or purpose. He'd tried to get back to her, but he never could. She sat trapped in the stillness of a snow globe, frozen but for her slow, even breaths. To have a glimpse was almost worse than not seeing her at all. He could never tell himself that she was in a better place. Her world had been frozen, and that's how it would always be.

He longed to reach out, to touch her hair. He'd tuck it behind her ear and lift up her chin. He'd ask if she was okay and then kiss her. She'd warm again. He'd embrace her, again feel her arms around his shoulders, the firmness of her back under his hands, the joy of her body on his. He'd hold her in an embrace until the walls of the cell fell away and they were somewhere else. He'd feel the rise and fall of her breath, and they'd share the warmth of fresh tears. But that was a dream. It never came.

She was always out of reach.

In some ways, that was better than the truth. He didn't want to imagine what the sheriff's office had found. She'd been frozen to the ice, trapped in a tableau of clawing desperation. He didn't want to imagine the angles of her elbows, the bareness of her fingers on the ice, the heaviness of wet clothing that, freezing, entombed her, or the pale, frosted pallor of her skin.

He didn't want to see it. It would poison his memory of her. He could never get it out of his mind. But it was as if the act of not seeing gave his mind free rein to imagine awful images, some worse than reality, but all reimagined again and again in the absence of the concrete truth. By not seeing her, his mind was trapped in a replay of projected horrors. And by not seeing her, he'd doomed himself to it. He closed his eyes and let the specter of death return to mist, let the image of his wife in the room return. That was her, a shadow of her, but not some ghastly thing. She was waiting.

He looked at the beckoning Superior water. This wasn't how he was going to go. Not right now. The ice and the water wanted him to give in. But that was not how they would be together again. Not by his hand.

So he sighed and stepped back from the edge, distancing himself from the chop of the waves. And he realized that he was exhausted, so despite the sun still floating in the sky, he decided to gather his things and prepare the sledge for another sleep in the cold. He would die another day. Maybe. Maybe tomorrow. Maybe.

CHAPTER TWENTY-SIX

He soon fell asleep.

He was aware of the ice, of the cold hard and the white. It was all around him and extended as far as he could see. The sun was shining from a spot just below the horizon, and it bathed everything in a muted glow. There were no shadows, just a gradual fall from light to dark in an endless field of bright white. He felt the wind and turned his back to it, hunching in his hood and burying his hands deep into pockets. Crystals of snow curled around him, driven by the wind, sparkling in the wan light like diamond dust.

He looked out at the horizon, at the endless ice. He had no pulk, no fishing equipment, and no chair. It was just him and the frozen expanse. It was beautiful. The view was sparse, devoid of any real feature, pure. He breathed slowly, felt the warmth of his parka in the space of his breath.

He felt safe.

But then he saw motion. It was a dot on the horizon, swaying. A shadow of white and gray. He watched it, curious and unsure. It dipped back and forth like a lone water bug on the glass of a pond. He watched as it grew and was followed by a hump of gray that bulged above the horizon. A black dot was joined by two others. Eyes. Below, huge paws flashed black with claws. His breath caught. His body tensed. Terror clutched his stomach, threatened to burst through his spine. The wolf looked far bigger than he'd ever imagined. It was coming straight for him, unwavering. Its body seemed to levitate with each step, but the shadows of nose and eyes were fixed on him.

The wolf must have smelled him. Why else would it be coming this way? Why else would it be out here but to follow its nose to the next meal? *Damned wind.*

It was headed for him, for food. He would be the food. He scrambled back, wanted to be far away. But all he could manage was a tiny scoot.

In long, efficient lopes, the wolf traversed the snow and ice. Twenty-five feet away, it stopped. It looked at him, its head like a snake's, mapping for a strike. Its eyes were penetrating, and he sensed thought behind it. The wolf was deciding. It looked at him, an unblinking gaze. Hugh was frozen.

The wolf's head lowered. It stepped sideways on a curved path, eyes steady, paws lifting effortlessly, silently closing the distance between them. Only a few steps away, it suddenly stopped. Its body curled tight, paws ready like a coiled spring aimed in his direction.

This is it, Hugh thought. The wolf was about to launch into him. The tightness was up in his throat. It was hard to breathe.

Then the spring released.

The wolf leaped up. At the top of its jump, its forepaws came together, shoulders flexed, and head lowered. It came down as an enormous hammer. The blow echoed across the ice like thunder. Hugh felt the surface shudder beneath him, and he reached out for balance. He scooted back and clambered to his feet.

The wolf was already back up, coiling its body tight to slam down again. It went up and down in quick blows. Again and again. Thump, thump, thump.

The ice trembled under Hugh's feet. And then he heard a crack, felt the ice give beneath him. He felt a tilt. The frozen sheet tipped toward the wolf. A new crack widened from its paws like a crescent moon, drawing a ragged arc all around Hugh. In an instant, he was on a floating berg, a tiny raft of unstable ice.

Still, the wolf kept pummeling his floating piece. The surface tossed under his feet. He twisted and swayed. The wolf was too strong, too heavy. Behind him, the ice lifted from the water, and Hugh slipped, slammed hard into the ice.

It was the fall that woke him up.

Hugh was trapped in a tight grip.

He was coiled in darkness, arms bound to his chest, feet hobbled. He twisted. Head back, he felt hard cold.

His body bucked and his prison jumped loose. He heard a hard *clack.* It was unmistakable: runners on ice. *The pulk*, he thought, *the sleeping bag.* He was twisted inside his cocoon. He tried to calm the overwhelming urge to free himself, took a deep breath. He was trapped. But more concerning was the motion—it was the bob and chop of ice on water, like a raft at the whim of the sea. And then he felt the slide of runners on ice. He was moving. The pulk was sliding. The ice was tilting.

He ripped at the zipper, clawed the fabric. Finding the lines, he tugged the knot. The pulk was still sliding. After two tugs, the line popped. He thrust his head and shoulders out and instinctively threw his bare hands to the ice to stop the slide. He dug into it with his fingernails. The living parts of his frostbitten hand howled with pain. There was no wolf. *A dream*, he thought. But the waking was more of a nightmare. The sight chilled him more than the bite of the cold at his fingers. He was surrounded by a mess of icebergs and water.

The floe had broken. He was on a raft just big enough for him and some of his gear. He was just a few feet from the ragged edge when suddenly his ice raft listed level and the pulk stopped. Hugh's breath caught. He held it in, worked to steady his nerves and the ice the same, as if letting go might make it all crumble.

The water, the ice, the sky: All were shades of gray. All the same, or soon to be.

On the next floe over, the bright colors and unnatural lines and shapes of his tip-up holes and rods bobbed up and down, incongruous in the emptiness.

And on the next was his fish, that monster. Even in the tumult, he marveled at it. It was so huge, so glorious, even on its little speck of ice. It moved now with the chop, as if reanimated in the afterlife. With the next list of the ice raft, his glorious trout slipped, splashing headfirst into the water. Down it went, the lake reclaiming its own.

Tears came and Hugh laughed at the preposterousness of it. He laughed at it even as his hands burned against the cold of the ice. His body was half in the pulk, his chest and shoulders at the mercy of the wind, and he laughed. How impossible and stupid it was, that fish. What had he imagined? That it would somehow matter that he'd caught it? Now, that fish was dead, and like the fish, he would soon slip into the cold water and the unknown below. He would be forever lost in the greatness of Lake Superior. He laughed at how it didn't matter. And he laughed that he'd thought it might.

That tightness in his chest, that tearing in his gut, was back. Any moment he'd tumble into the frigid water too.

His body tingled.

Once he was in the water, his body would slow with the cold within minutes. It would pull back, sacrifice tissue for limbs, limbs for organs, and then organs for brain. And then it would give up. With that, he'd stop kicking and slip under. It would be a silent farewell. One minute, he would be above the surface, breathing. The next, he'd be in the dark below, his lungs filling with water as he sank to an unknown grave where his body would stay forever, preserved by the cold as if frozen in time. The thought chilled him. It was terrifying, a horrible and lonely end.

He pulled himself out of the pulk, the pains in his hands and his chest and his face blossoming anew, and crawled toward the center of his raft of ice. His home was disintegrating. Even as he watched, the raft was breaking, shards flaking off the edge like a cracking mirror. It shuddered under him, and he watched as more calved off and drifted away, dragged on by the wind and tumult of the sea. He again felt the ice bending beneath him. Cracks radiated from the triple-augered hole nearby. Water pooled out and the inky black expanded.

He heard a thick *clunk*, and the dark line of a fracture appeared under his pulk. He moved back, scrambled to his feet. The edges of the crack spread wider. Hugh watched as the sled shifted, pivoting around the shadow growing beneath as it was pulled from two directions at once. Beyond the sled, great pieces of ice broke and rolled in the water, tumbling end over end, their glassy underbellies turning to the sky.

The pulk bridged the crack until it was too wide, and the end of the sled slipped off the ice, the tip slapping the water with a splash. The rest of it slid off, and the whole thing pitched on the surface like a miniature ship. The iceberg next to it, with the pile of his gear, rolled left, then right, then back toward him. He watched as his remaining possessions spilled into the water. The sleeping bag floated like foam until the frying pan tumbled onto it, the two disappearing into the inky depths below. The last of the sinking mass caught the edge of the auger, catapulting it. The sheath popped off the bit and it slammed against the ice before dropping from view. Shifting ice bobbed against the sled, pushing the end under. Water filled the inside, and all its teetering suddenly stopped as if it had been stunned by the cold. In a moment, it was gone, leaving a scatter of flotsam on the surface.

Hugh watched in stunned silence. He sensed the depth of the water underneath him, hundreds of feet to the bottom.

But he had no more time to think.

The ice tilted under his feet like a broken sidewalk. Water sloshed on the surface, slick and slanted. His mukluks skittered out from under him. He backpedaled, feet searching for purchase, arms out for balance.

He faltered, fell back hard, the ice as immovable against his bones as a block of granite. His ribs were on fire.

He cried out with pain and slid down the ice, legs first into the water. It bit at him with cold, and he gasped. Twisting, he curled his mittens around the lip of ice and pulled. The berg rolled toward him. Off-balance, pushed by the ice, he tipped back. He tried to stop it, tried to keep up with the ice, but it had too much mass, too much momentum, a meteor tumbling through space. A lobe of the berg swung up out of the water and then slammed down on his shoulder. It didn't stop, kept pushing, and suddenly Hugh was underwater, then deeper still by the roll of ice.

The cold enveloped him. His ears popped. His skin burned. His muscles ached. He yearned to go back. Instinct told him to reach for the surface, that quicksilver chaos of waves and bobbing icebergs. Then he realized how calm it was beneath the surface. His body stilled, and he felt suddenly warm. It felt good. The roiling of ice in water, the rush of wind and its frigid bite on the air, its howl and whistle through the tumult, was all gone. There was only that motion above and the bubbles rising around him. Everything else was stillness. It was silent too, a kind of peace. Hugh paused, soaked it in. He wasn't sure if he should return to the surface, to the maelstrom—to fight and survive, or to embrace the quiet peace and pressure of this watery grave. To go up was nothing but death and pain. To go below was death and peace.

And while he floated in that moment, in that bardo between worlds, he noticed a shadow. It appeared from the deep. *A fish?* he thought. *No, much too large.* It was an apparition, a smudge of dark in the greenish blackness. It grew until he recognized the shape. The shadow formed into head, shoulders, torso, and legs.

A mermaid? he thought. The idea was both laughable and completely plausible. It didn't so much swim toward him as float, borne on some unknown current. *A ghost.* The light was so dim that the figure lacked definition until it was only an arm's length away.

Sarah, he thought, and though he hadn't spoken a word, she heard him and smiled.

This wasn't the apparition of his nightmares—the cold, waxy corpse that plagued his subconscious. This was the real Sarah. They were together in the water. She hadn't aged, looked the same as when he'd last seen her. Her brown hair floated behind her, silhouetting the pale skin of her face. He brought a hand toward her, ran a thumb along her cheek. It was soft and smooth and warm. She leaned into his hand, closed her eyes, and he could see her soften as she held his touch.

He felt something let go. It was a tension of years, of a lifetime. In that moment, he imagined the life they'd had and the life they'd lost. He remembered what it had been to feel real love, and he felt it then again. He closed his eyes, remembered her laugh and her smile, and those moments when they'd taken each other in their arms wholly and without any perception of either one of them, just that feeling of being together. And it was all real again.

He felt her hand wrap around his, and he opened his eyes. A soft, knowing look as if to say she knew what he was feeling and that it was okay. She held that look, and then deep creases crossed her brow. She gently pulled his hand from her cheek.

She slowly shook her head, her mouth formed a thin line, and her face softened. He felt her voice and the words *Oh, Hugh, I'm so sorry.* She took him in her arms then and kissed his forehead. *I've missed you.*

She held there, and he felt the soft warmth of her lips on skin that had missed the feeling for so long. She released the kiss, and in his heart, he heard her say, *I love you.*

But then she pulled back and looked into his eyes. She gripped his arms. *This isn't it, though. There's more for you to do*, she said. *You have to go back.*

She held his gaze a moment longer and then thrust him up, back toward the surface, and she disappeared once more in the deep.

He felt the rush of water. The cold of it filled his clothes anew. Then his head broke the surface, and he gasped, the cold air burning his throat and lungs, the frigid wind biting at his scalp. His body heaved as it pulled in fresh oxygen. As he treaded water and swallowed air, his arms and legs ached with the effort in the cold, already beginning to ignore his commands.

He looked around, tried to find something to hold on to, to help him stay afloat. Behind him and a few feet off was an iceberg. He pulled clumsily toward it, not knowing why, but knowing now that he couldn't let go and give in. This berg was more solid than the last, and he gripped it tight, but the ice slipped from his hands. Remembering the picks, he felt for them at the end of the strings. They were there. Gripping each tight, he slammed them home on the ice, chips flying as they bit into the block.

Finally able to pull his head clear of the choppy water, he worked to catch his breath. But between the submersion, the cold, and the effort, it was almost impossible. There was no such thing as enough air. And so, he hung on, shook the water from his face, and focused on taking deep breaths.

His ears rang, a buzz interrupted only by the steady and quick thump of his heart. He wondered at what fate he'd been returned to. What could possibly change from here.

Then another sound. A low hum. He couldn't place it at first, but it steadily grew louder until he recognized it.

It was an engine.

CHAPTER TWENTY-SEVEN

Trooper 9 was a top-of-the-line Duluth-made, propeller-driven aircraft capable of achieving 180 knots. The cabin seated up to four individuals: a pilot in command, a sensor operator, and up to two observers. It responded out of the Twin Cities to assist with motor vehicle enforcement and monitoring, high-speed pursuits, and search and rescue missions. For today's mission, two of the seats were vacant. Isaac Dahnle was the pilot in command at the left seat. To his right was John Chance. Chance would be operating the optics for most of the flight and would keep comms with Search Command. Much of the observation was conducted with the unit's state-of-the-art imaging package.

With advanced daytime and infrared camera capabilities, *Trooper 9* had proven itself over and over again during operations across the state and the region. On this cold January day over Lake Superior, Dahnle and Chance had been working through sectors north of the Apostle Islands when they were pulled from the mission to find two missing kids in a swamp near Hibbing. Reluctantly, they left one search to help with another and turned west for shore.

After they had located and circled the huddled pair of kids and watched as ground teams reached them and brought them to safety, *Trooper 9* turned for the Duluth airport to refuel. The stop was brief but allowed the men an opportunity to stretch their legs and congratulate one another on their successful find.

Refreshed, they climbed back into the leather-lined cockpit. It had been cold outside, a light dusting of snow carried on the stiff wind, but with the doors shut, the cockpit was warm. They donned headsets and ran through the preflight check.

After a short taxi, the crew was cleared for takeoff.

Dahnle opened the throttle and released the brake. The cabin was surprisingly quiet as the engine opened up and the small craft accelerated. It reached takeoff velocity quickly and was suddenly off the runway, turning right to make the approach to the lake. Beneath them, snow-covered trees and swamp seemed to stretch to the horizon. They flew toward loosely packed suburbs and the dense hillside neighborhoods near the endless expanse of the lake, the steely frame of the Duluth Aerial Lift Bridge in miniature silhouette.

Chance keyed his radio and spoke into the headset mic. "*Trooper 9*, Search Command on STAC4."

After a short pause, the radio clicked, and a voice came through their headsets. "Go ahead *Trooper 9*."

"*Trooper 9* is in the air, nearing your position now and headed to resume our search of grid A12," Chance said.

"Command copies. *Trooper 9*, be advised, there are other aircraft engaged in the search," the voice said. "To deconflict the airspace, we'll maintain your previous altitude assignment: You are assigned twenty-five hundred to five thousand feet MSL. We have a rotor wing operating below two thousand feet MSL. That's the coast guard Dolphin, and they'll be searching near your area of operations. We have six thousand to ten thousand MSL assigned to an incoming C-130 that's roughly two hours out."

Chance tapped the numbers into the mapping system and then

keyed the mic. "Good copy," he said. "*Trooper 9* will be operating from two thousand five hundred to five thousand feet MSL."

"Happy hunting," the voice said.

The pilots knew their assignment, knew their sectors, where they'd left off, and what was remaining. The predominant theory for their part of the search was that McLaren had been able to sustain himself on the ice and that he was riding it out into the lake. But hope was dwindling. The survival theory got thinner with each passing hour, and most of the team in the command center and in the field were absorbing the reality that they probably wouldn't be making a rescue. It had already been several days, and it had been so damn cold. Not to mention, the waves had made a mess of the ice. Most of the wind and ice floe dispersion models pointed to the ice floe having reached a wide swath at a point on the lake between the Apostle Islands on Wisconsin's south shore of the lake and the town of Silver Bay on Minnesota's north shore. It could be farther or closer. In any case, the median estimate was that the subject had drifted between sixty-five and seventy-five miles from where he'd started in Duluth. That would be a hell of a float on a crumbling pack.

As *Trooper 9* approached their section on the map, a square labeled A12 that lay north of the Apostle Islands, they kept the cameras on and watched through the windows for any sign. Sometimes, you're as likely to make a find on the way somewhere as once you arrive. When the GPS showed them arriving at A12, Chance keyed the radio. "*Trooper 9*, Command," he said.

"Go for Command," the voice said.

"We are on station at grid A12, beginning our search," said Chance.

"Copy that, *Trooper 9*, beginning search of A12," said the voice.

With each sector ten miles on a side, they'd be able to achieve effective coverage of around five grids before they had to return for a refuel. The plane arced along an invisible track, following the preplanned route on the map and an arbitrary set of lines and corners that had no relation to the natural world. The map traced a line behind the plane, and Chance controlled the thermal camera, keeping it at a wide angle to scan and tightening in as he found formations of ice that needed a closer look.

The pilots were connected by an intercom system that allowed them to speak naturally with each other without using the push-to-talk function required for the radio. When not in an active mission area, they used this to converse like the two longtime partners they were, checking in on the weekend, on their kids and general thoughts about life. When they were *on*, though, the chatter died and they were all focus.

Dahnle had been quiet, focused on the aircraft and its controls and navigation, but as they transitioned from sector A12 to A11, he spoke. "You see how the ice is getting closer together down there?" he said. The interspersed icebergs they'd been seeing had seemed to coalesce, forming a rough patchwork on the water.

"Yeah, I see it," said Chance.

"I wonder if we're getting closer to the Duluth floe," said Dahnle. His eyes went from the water to the gauges to the airspace in front of them. His left hand held the flight control stick near the cabin wall, which danced with the subtle nuance of the wind. *Trooper 9*, though certainly a smooth flier, was not immune to the perturbations of the wind and was in constant motion during much of this mission. Dahnle's hand danced back and forth to compensate and adjust. The plane rocked side to side with the gusts, rose and fell with an odd, syncopated rhythm. Down at the surface, the lake was a dark riffle of water tormented by that same wind. Between the fragments of ice and the rolling whitecaps was the dark of the roiling water. Lake Superior was whipping up, and the waves were beginning to stack now, growing in size.

"Looks like the wave action is actually breaking up the ice even more," said Dahnle.

"Yeah," said Chance. "That doesn't bode well for our guy."

"No, it doesn't," said Dahnle. "I'm going to throttle up so we can cover more ground."

"Copy that," said Chance.

With his right hand, Dahnle pushed the throttle control. They felt the extra push into the backs of their seats as the engine's RPMs climbed.

Chance keyed the radio. "*Trooper 9*, Search Command."

After a beat, a voice came on the radio and said, "*Trooper 9*."

Chance gave their position, heading, and speed. "We're encountering more ice density here, which makes us think we might be encountering the Duluth floe, but be advised that wind and wave activity appears to be increasing in the area and breaking the ice up even further."

"Command copies all, *Trooper 9*," the voice said. "Thanks for the update."

Chance adjusted the controls on the camera, zoomed in and out to find the balance between the right level of legibility and coverage area. Satisfied, he set to his visual scanning. The infrared camera showed nothing hot, only the cold gray of ice, with pockets of shadow where it was even colder still, all played against the chop of turbid water.

As *Trooper 9* made its southbound turn on grid A10, Chance noticed something on the screen. On the black and white of the thermal, it was like more ice, but the angles were different, didn't match the random geometry he'd been staring at for the entire search. He blinked and looked again, lifted a finger to point at the screen and help him fixate on it. He pushed a button at the control to mark the spot, then glanced out the cockpit window. The view through the pane was murkier than on the screen. He zoomed the camera closer, and the angles stood out even more.

"Target, right," he said through the intercom.

"Copy," said Dahnle, instantly rolling the aircraft a few degrees into a nodal turn to the right.

"I've got a possible debris field," said Chance. He zoomed the camera further still. With the slow arc of the plane, the image took on the familiar, supernatural rotation. Chance bent to the screen as if it were an extension of his own senses. And he could feel that familiar rush, that spike in adrenaline, as the whole world seemed to align into this one defined moment and action. After days of looking at a tableau of organic emptiness, he made out unnatural forms: corners, slow curves, bundles.

Then something else came into view at the edge of water and a berg.

"Holy shit," said Chance. "I've got a heat signature."

Chance looked at the screen again, then the map. He keyed the microphone. "*Trooper 9*, Command, target in sight, he's in the water, standby for location." Command acknowledged, and Chance read off the coordinates on his screen.

"Good copy, *Trooper 9*," the voice said. "Coast guard Dolphin is near your AO."

Then another voice came over the air. "Coast guard Dolphin copies all," it said. "We're four minutes out."

CHAPTER TWENTY-EIGHT

The sound of the motor came to him in waves, gradually overpowering the sound of the wind and the water tossing around him. *Is it the search plane?* he thought. No, this was different. This was more throaty, a rumble. *Something else . . .*

And then it appeared like a flash on the horizon: orange, a spear of fire among the gray.

The rumble became a roar. He saw the dark line of a spinning rotor, the aggressive swoop of fuselage, and the keen dark eyes of the cockpit windshield. It was a helicopter, all orange and black, and it was moving fast. He could see the side too, the large cabin doors shut against the cold.

It wasn't quite heading toward him. It was flying past him, a glancing blow off to the right, as if in a show of force to demonstrate it was there, taunting him with how close it had come.

Then it was heading away. Off toward the other horizon.

Hugh's breath quickened. *No, no, no,* he thought, *don't go!* He fought up, kicked, and threw his arms up, waving them wildly. His picks slipped from his shoulders and floated away.

"Hey . . ." he said, his voice meek and weak. It felt foreign to him, and he coughed to find it again. Taking a deep, agonizing breath, he started anew. "Hey!" he yelled, now a clear bellow that pierced the air. "Hey! Over here! I'm here!" His arms swung in a wide arc, and he kicked to stay at the surface.

Even with this burst of energy, the sudden effort, he could feel his body succumbing. The wave of his arms was slowing, and his legs felt heavy. He tried, and his voice turned to a desperate scream. He was spent. That had been it, his last effort. The cold was soaking through to his core, and he was shutting down.

Even so, the helicopter kept on, true to its course. Unwavering and unstoppable. They had missed him, and now he would die.

But then it tilted.

The flat disk of the rotors tipped into an ellipse, and he could see the top of the craft. A sharp right turn. The sound from the rotors and engine thunked down suddenly to a chunky growl.

They had seen him.

Hugh felt a wave of emotion shoot like lightning from his scalp to his toes. He nearly dropped below the surface with the abruptness of his realization. They were turning toward him. They knew he was there, and they were coming toward him. "Oh my god," he cried, and his eyes clouded with tears.

In a moment, he felt the hurricane of wind from the rotors. The roar was deafening. So much after such silence. The intense winds and the cacophony obliterated everything. The ice bounced wildly around him, the water punished to trembling flatness by the rotor wash. He looked up at bright, flashing lights. The huge orange helicopter looked fixed, motionless above him. He saw the curve of helmets peeking out the side door.

His jaw stilled its quaking, and his legs slowed their staccato kick. He felt the spasm of muscle. He couldn't keep kicking, couldn't float. His body was failing.

He looked up again at the chaos of machine and wind and noise above him. A pair of swimming fins suddenly appeared next to the fuselage. A moment later, with a splash, a figure was in the water. It was the shape of a man, but the man was hidden, covered head to toe in a red survival suit, sparkling with reflective tape, with a hood that wrapped around dive goggles and a snorkel mouthpiece.

A cable appeared next to the figure in the water. At the end was a padded loop, as if to moor a boat to a pier. Hugh's eyes followed the dangling cable to its end up in the sky. The bright lights on the helicopter made it hard to see the crew, but he could just make out the motions of one leaning out the door, one hand on the cable as if he alone were guiding it. Hugh squinted and wiped spray from his eyes.

The world was slowing now, and motion blurred it as if painted in oil.

The man in the water pulled hard toward Hugh, taking up the loop on the way. In a few short strokes, he wrapped a strong arm around Hugh's torso and in one motion guided the loop over his shoulders and under his arms.

He sensed the swimmer making adjustments and then felt the wind increase, heard a roar from above. He gave in, and felt his weight pull on the man and the machine. Suddenly the loop was pulling at his chest, lifting him from the water. His ribs ached, masked by the cold and rush of adrenaline. The sudden gravity on his drenched clothes felt like they might rip from his body, and as he rose, he felt the chill of wind and rotor wash whipping against him. It was bitingly cold.

He dangled, looked down at the lake, at the scattered flotsam of his floe and the remaining bits of his gear still afloat. The world spun, and he looked to the horizon to keep his equilibrium. There was nothing but lake as far as he could see. At the edge was unending water, touched by the deep blue of coming twilight and the last hint of heavy pink as the sun set to the west.

The roar of the engine and the thump of the rotor crescendoed. It was impossibly loud. The noise obliterated everything. And then it was joined by the whine of the winch, and he was being pulled sideways. The side of the fuselage appeared, with a helmeted figure at the cable, one gloved hand guiding it from above, the other pulling Hugh in through the open door.

More hands guided him in, laid him down, and unclipped him from the loop. Arms and legs and gear enveloped him, and the door slid shut.

The helicopter banked, and he felt the pull of acceleration. There was a flurry of domed helmets and gloved hands and exposure suits around him. One man prepared a needle for an IV. Another wrapped him in wool and Mylar.

The world was still swirling.

Then he noticed the man from the water, snorkel aside to reveal a thin mustache, mouth, and chin. The man leaned back on his heels and, in one motion, ripped the plastic clips from a grip of instant hot pads. He shook the pouches back and forth, peeled back the blankets, and stuffed the packets, already warming, under Hugh's armpits, at his chest, and between his legs.

"Hugh McLaren?" the rescue swimmer said, yelling to be heard over the din.

"Yes," Hugh managed, jaw clumsy, chattering.

"We're going to get you home," the man yelled, tightening the blanket around his shoulders.

"How . . ." Hugh said, his voice trailing off, breathless. "How did you know I was out here?"

"Your daughter, sir," said the sailor.

And at that, he realized that Lauren had gotten his message. Moreover, it had meant something. His eyes filled with tears, and he lay back on the helicopter floor.

When he opened them again, there was another figure, another patient he somehow hadn't noticed behind the other crew. She seemed to come and go with the light. He could tell it was a woman by her silhouette against the helicopter's navigation lights glowing outside. She sat wrapped in a blanket, wet hair draped across her shoulders. She was angled toward him, but her face was hidden in darkness. Then the light shifted, and he could see her, see the curve of her cheek, and the light of her eyes. She was looking at him too, and he recognized her. And she was smiling.

CHAPTER TWENTY-NINE

The call came when Lauren was pushing a cart at the Plaza Grocery, when she was already overwhelmed by the Technicolor produce, a stark contrast to the bitter wind and blowing snow and the drab emptiness of her father's house. The call was unexpected, startling her with a loud ringtone instead of the quiet vibration she was used to. She nearly dropped the phone twice pulling it from her purse. The screen showed "No Caller ID" in big white letters.

"Hello?" she said. "Yes, that's me . . . Mr. Calvin, yes, hello," she said, recognizing his voice. She could picture the man in his uniform, imagined him standing at the bank of computer screens in the command truck.

"Yes, hi, thank you for picking up," he said, but then his voice began to cut in and out, so she could only catch every few words. "Ms. Cox . . . some . . . news . . . it's . . ." She filled in the gaps and felt her stomach drop. This was it. They'd found him, and it wasn't good—or worse, they were calling off the search, and she would never find the closure she so desperately wanted. She pressed her eyes shut and plugged her other ear. "Next steps . . . report . . . sorry . . . sooner . . ." It was too garbled.

"Mr. Calvin," she said. She pulled the phone away and looked at the screen, the broken words still whispering through the earpiece. One bar of signal strength, then none, then back to one. "Shit," she said, bringing the phone back to her ear. "Mr. Calvin, wait, hold on. I've got a bad signal, and I can't quite hear you."

She grabbed her purse and turned from the cart, speeding away in long strides, hoping for a better connection near the door. Her face was flushed; she shook her head. She was suddenly thrown into a flurry of feelings.

"Can't . . . Cox?" the voice said.

She held the phone in front of her, watching the bars flicker off and on. She swore again. The doors opened with a *whoosh*, and she stepped outside. She winced against sudden cold, covered her face from the wind and the snow that whipped from drifts piled high around the lot. She looked at the screen. Call failed.

"Ah damnit!" she said. The phone showed no bars. A couple of paces forward, it climbed to two, then added a third. She pressed the Call Back icon and held the phone to her ear, turning her back to the wind, wrapping her opened coat around her. Instead of a ring, she heard a garbled female voice saying the call couldn't be completed as dialed. She thumbed the End button and held the phone to her chest, looking around the lot for some shelter where she could wait for a call back. Other than a few cars and the narrow trunks of streetlight poles, the lot was empty. The sky was the deep blue of twilight and quickly darkening toward night; the lights were on. They cast pools of amber glow around them and sparkled the blowing snow.

Her phone chimed again, and she answered as quickly as she could.

"Hello? Mr. Calvin?" she said.

"Yes, Ms. Cox, can you hear me?" he said.

"Yes, yes, I was in bad signal and could only hear a word here and there, and it . . ." she said, turning from the unrelenting wind and suddenly stumbling on the worry swirling in her mind. "It didn't sound good."

"Ms. Cox, I'm sorry about that, but I actually have good news," he said.

She paused, pushed the phone harder into her ear. "Sorry, did you say *good* news?"

"Yes," he said. "Ms. Cox, we found your father, and he's alive."

Her body straightened, as if the wind and the cold had suddenly vanished. Calvin was still talking, but Lauren's mind had shut out his voice momentarily. She blinked into the darkening night. A sudden twinge of electricity ran down her spine, tingled through her arms and legs, and then rose up through her chest. Her eyes welled, and she pressed her other hand over her mouth.

"Ms. Cox?" he said. "Can you still hear me?"

"Yes, yes," she said. "I'm just . . . you found my dad alive?"

"Yes, ma'am," he said. "The coast guard is flying him to Duluth as we speak."

"Oh my god," she said. "I can't . . ."

"I understand, ma'am," he said. "You can go to the ED on Fourth and Fourth. Tell them the situation, and you should be able to see him once he's stable."

"ED?" she asked. "And you said . . . is he okay?"

"Sorry, ED is emergency department. And he's alive and conscious, was talking with the crew and in good spirits. It's about as good an outcome we could hope for. He's damn lucky . . . They actually hoisted him out of the water. Damn lucky they were there and got eyes on him when they did. He must not have been in very long, and honestly, it's a bit of a miracle," he said. "But you have to understand: He's been through an ordeal, they're working to warm him up from some significant exposure, and he has a number of injuries. The medics on the chopper didn't note any immediate life threats, but they'll continue to assess him throughout the flight and at the hospital. The folks there know what they're doing. They'll get him the care he needs."

"Okay," Lauren said. "Thank you, Mark. I can't say it enough: thank you to you and your team. I'm going to go there now."

"Copy that," he said. "We'll let them know you're coming."

It was a short drive down Superior Street, past her father's house, then up the hillside on Fourth Street to the emergency room. She parked at a meter and crossed the steep avenue to the guarded entrance. Through the holes in a glass partition, she explained who she was, that her father had been rescued from the lake, and that she needed to see him. The guard listened, told her they'd been expecting her, and opened the door, but she got only as far as the waiting room before she was told to have a seat.

She watched the hands on the wall clock turn around and around. People came and went, some in agony, some in quiet suffering, still others agitated and stumbling. One by one, the chosen were plucked from the room while Lauren waited. Finally, a nurse stepped in and called her name. Lauren followed her back to a consultation room and learned that her father had been stabilized and transferred to the ICU but that she could see him.

A warren of hallways and elevators led to the burn unit. They walked past the glass walls of patient rooms with people broken, healing, and dying. She finally reached his room, and the nurse left her at the door.

The lights in the room were dim, just enough to see the towers of monitors, tubes and fluids, carts and computers. The corner room had most of the curtains drawn shut over the nearly floor-to-ceiling windows that made up two of the walls. Through the open ones, Lauren could see the seemingly endless expanse of Lake Superior, touched by the silver sparkle of moonlight on the wind-cursed water.

Lauren paused, closed her eyes, and took a deep breath. A privacy curtain divided the room, and she couldn't see the bed, still hadn't seen her father. She had yet to cross that threshold back into his life. She stepped forward and peeled back the curtain. There in the bed, that domineering presence she'd known as a kid was something else entirely—just a small old man in a huge room of lights and tubes and monitors.

Most of his body was covered in a big inflated blanket, with plastic ports coupled to ductwork and a heating unit humming near the bed. One arm was wrapped in bulky bandaging that started above the shoulder and went all the way down to his hand so that just the tips of his fingers were exposed. These were dark, the nails a startling ivory against the shine of puffed, purpled skin. She took a sharp breath and looked away. His head was wrapped in bandages bulked with dressings at his chin and forehead. His face was sunken and chapped, his cheeks dark. His eyes were closed, and if it wasn't for the monitors displaying his vitals, she could have mistaken him for dead instead of sleeping.

She slowly crossed over to him, steps soft so as not to break the silence, her eyes filling with tears as the weight of the search and the worry and the decades seemed to build up to this moment. She knelt at his bedside, reached out as if to touch him, but her hand went instead to cover her mouth. She was overwhelmed. She tried to speak, but no words came, and she silently mouthed the word *Dad*.

His chin rose with a deep breath, and he opened his eyes, turned toward her.

"Lauren," he said, and he smiled in a way she hadn't seen since she was a girl. His smile held, and then she saw it begin to quiver. "You came," he said.

She suddenly felt the weight of the years. Felt it on her chest and surrounding her body like iron. She was dizzy, realizing she had been holding her breath. Not for just this moment—she'd been doing it for so long, guarding herself since she was that little girl. It was armor, and she realized for the first time in a very long time, she could let it go. She exhaled and felt that tension leave her body. She could breathe. After so much time, a lifetime, now they were suddenly together, and under these dramatic circumstances. And in that perspective, she felt the distillation of things: This was her dad. He was irreplaceable. He was her only father. He had been gone, but here he was.

"Lauren, you saved me," he said. "Just like your mother. She saved me too. I can't say how, but I know it was her. You're like her in so many ways. She lives on in you."

In that moment, Lauren felt her too, like the glow of summer sunshine. Memories of her mother had, for so long, brought nothing but pain, from not only the loss of that person but also the loss of what once was and what could never be. But now, for the first time in forever, those memories turned her mouth into a smile. Despite the cold dry air of the hospital and the winter night outside, that glow radiated down Lauren's neck and across her shoulders, filling her to the core.

She took her father's good hand in hers, and somehow, things felt all right. They were all going to be okay.

EPILOGUE

Lauren leaned on the rim of the pedestal sink and stared down at the cold water swirling into the drain. Again, she put her hands under the water and rubbed the cold on her neck, the chill a balm against the nervousness that burned there. She looked in the mirror, saw the flush in her cheeks, the slow curls of her dark-blond hair so carefully rolled earlier in the day. She took a steadying breath, let it out slowly. But in her eyes, she found the question that was imploding in her chest.

How am I going to do this?

The room outside the bathroom was stuffy, dated wallpaper atop dark wooden wainscoting. A few people milled about, mostly waiting to hang their overcoats. They nodded to her, silently mouthing greetings, and she did the same. She crossed the room, skirted past the entrance to avoid several more people just arriving. She wanted to be small, unnoticeable, didn't want to launch into the same conversation with every person, with every group.

In the next room, she found her husband and their two kids. She walked up to him, and they leaned into a quick kiss before she bent down and took a kid in each arm and gave them both a peck on the cheek.

"Hey, kiddos," she said, smiling at each one in turn. "How ya doing?"

They leaned back and looked at her. Her son answered first. "I don't want to be here," he said, his face scrunched up.

"I know, buddy," Lauren said. "I know. It's hard, but it's important, and then we'll be done."

"Mommy," her daughter said, rising on tiptoes in her tiny patent-leather shoes. "Mommy, I don't know why we have to be here. Grandpa's not even here."

Lauren sighed and bent down so their foreheads touched. "I know, sweetheart, it's confusing," she said, leaning back to look at her again and straightening one of the girl's stray curls. "But he knows you're here, right? And that's as important as anything else."

"But how does he know?" her daughter asked.

"He knows, sweetie. Look, I know this is hard for both of you, but you're being so patient and will just need to be a bit longer, okay?" Lauren said.

She looked at each and waited for an acknowledgment. After a curt nod from the boy and an exaggerated up-and-down from her daughter, she stood and took their hands. She turned back to her husband, a look of apology across her face. She took a breath and was about to speak when he interrupted her.

"It's good that we're here, Lauren," he said. "This is important. You and your dad were apart for so long, and it's okay if it's not easy."

She nodded and felt her eyes welling up as he spoke. She tried to stop the tears from snowballing further, blinked her eyes in short bursts like the beat of butterfly wings, and inhaled sharply. "I know. I know. You're right," she said. "And it feels right to be here. But it sucks too."

"I know," he said. "But it's better than just leaving it like it was, right?"

"Yeah," she said, then scoffed. "Yeah, that's for sure."

Out of the corner of her eye, she caught sight of someone stepping into the room, and after her brain had registered recognition, she turned to get a better look.

"Oh god . . ." she said, and she stepped away from the kids and her husband. "Jason! I didn't think you'd come!" She embraced her brother, then stepped back to look at his navy-blue uniform, the shine of the buttons, and the stripes of his service ribbons. "Jeez, look at you. I'm so happy you're here."

"Hey, sis," he said, thrown a little off-balance by the hug and sudden affection but embracing her nonetheless. It had been a long time. "I was on the fence, but I'm here."

She smiled and nodded back at him. "Well, I'm glad you are," she said. "Come say hi to the kids."

They crossed the room, and Lauren reintroduced him. "Kids, this is your uncle Jason. Do you remember him?" she said. Her children shifted uncomfortably.

He leaned in to shake the hand of Lauren's husband, then crouched down to eye level with the boy and girl.

"Hey guys, it's been a while," he said, careful to give them enough space. "It's good to see you. Don't worry about my costume. I'm not a cop or anything. See, you two are dressed up too." He gestured at their fancy shoes, the boy's miniature suit, and her modest dress, all black. They paused, looked at his uniform, at their own outfits, and then nodded.

Jason stood and looked at his sister. "Holy shit, they've gotten big," he said, quiet enough for them not to hear.

"I know," she said. "I swear every time I look at a picture of them, I'm like, what happened?"

"Well, I guess this'll be it, huh?" Jason said, more quietly. "Are you ready?"

Lauren looked at him, then down at the kids and at the room, at the small collection of photos spread on the tables.

"I think so," she said. "I guess I'm more ready than I've been in a long time."

He looked at her, watched her expression, one both guarded and filled with the weight of what she now carried. He lifted his chin in a slow nod. "I'm glad you got some time with him, sis," he said.

"Me too," she said. "I still can't believe it." She paused, shook her head.

Jason sighed. "Yeah, well, someone his age and all that shit out there, it's not a surprise his body couldn't take it, even if he hadn't been sick before," he said, and he shook his head, looked around the room, then back at his sister. "So that's what finally did it, huh, pneumonia?"

"Yep," she said, and she closed her eyes, worked to clear the images in the hospital from her mind, their conversations, and then his quick decline. "It was all just too much."

Jason pulled her into a hug. "I'm sorry," he said. "But I'm proud of you, sis. And he would be too."

"I know," she said, wiping an escaping tear. She nodded, and her mouth pressed into a small accepting smile. "He said as much."

He smiled back, squeezed her shoulder, and wrapped her in another strong hug. When they stepped apart, Jason fell in with his nephew and niece next to their father. Lauren walked ahead. They found the door to the small chapel at the back of the building. It could maybe fit one hundred people with every seat filled. It wouldn't be close to capacity today, but there were more attendees than any of them had expected. The room was a cross section of a life: people from work, neighbors and other fishermen, staff from the hospital, and a cluster of uniforms from the rescue.

At one end, near the modest stage and the podium with the microphone and the bible, was a simple wooden box. It was varnished in golden oak, a weathered bronze plate affixed to the front, with raised letters across it that read, "Hugh Allen McLaren."

Lauren looked at the box, at the tableau of people, and sighed. How different this day would have been only a month ago.

The officiant went to the podium and greeted everyone, found verses of scripture, and shared his own scripted words. There was no music, no reading together. It was quiet and subdued, as Hugh would have wanted it. And then it was time for Lauren.

She stepped to the lectern, adjusted the small microphone, and removed a folded paper from the inside pocket of her jacket. The room was quiet, and the crinkle of the papers as she laid them flat seemed to fill the space.

She looked up, took a steadying breath, and then began.

ACKNOWLEDGMENTS

This book wouldn't be here without the help, support, and insight of many people. I'd like to extend my thanks to my agent, Philip, for representing the book. To Marilyn and the team at Blackstone—thank you for believing in it and making it happen. And to my editor, William, for helping this story grow and evolve into something real. To my mom, Phyllis, for her thoughtfulness and listening ear through so many edits and rewrites. To my friends and colleagues who helped with research, friends who shared experiences and insights on ice fishing, and those I sat with on the ice, thank you. Thanks to Viann for discussions on psychology and trauma. Thanks to colleagues from the St. Louis County Sheriff's Rescue Squad, for breaking the ice together and for being sounding boards on long drives and late nights as I worked through drafts and technical questions—specifically Rick, Jarrid, Don, and Max: Your feedback, perspectives, and experiences helped to enrich this story with authenticity. And to everyone who supported me with excitement about the story, or who shared ideas and thoughts, I truly appreciate you.

Special thanks to my family. To Orson and Ayla—your curiosity and joy are inspiring. And to Lacey—thank you for your keen storytelling eye and edits, but especially for your patience as I dove into this world.

Lastly, I'm grateful to have spent a lot of time with Lake Superior as I imagined and worked through drafts and edits. Mornings on the shore, subzero temperatures, spectacular sunrises, and the lake's many moods helped to inspire this story.

Q&A WITH THE AUTHOR

Q: How did you come up with the concept for *The Ice on the Lake*?

A: I first started thinking of this story in February of 2021. I was a member of the St. Louis County Rescue Squad at the time, and we received a page for twenty-six anglers who had been on the ice when it broke free from land. They were adrift on Lake Superior and moving away from shore. I was unable to respond, but later I stood on the cliffs at Leif Erikson Park and watched as my colleagues in the airboat were motoring back toward the Aerial Lift Bridge when they abruptly turned to one of the floes of ice. They picked up the one remaining stranded fisherman. He had been walking to the other side of the bay, from Duluth, Minnesota, to the distant shores of Wisconsin, miles away, where the enormous floe was still pivoting against the shore. I thought, *What if no one knew he was out there?* That was the initial inspiration for *The Ice on the Lake.*

Q: Your first book was a memoir. What made you choose fiction this time?

A: I wanted to write something that wasn't about me and also didn't have the responsibility and emotional burden that comes with telling another person's true story. So I decided to see where my imagination would take me. As with any fiction, a lot of fact and experience went into creating *The Ice on the Lake*, and I think that helped make it vivid and believable. That freedom, though, can be hugely challenging because it's all on you as the author to make it happen, to make it real, and to make it compelling. I hope I've achieved that and more.

Q: There are a lot of challenging themes explored in this text. Where did these come from?

A: When I began writing *The Ice on the Lake*, it wasn't necessarily going to become a book. I didn't know what it would be, but I wanted to explore this story. As I was writing, I was also going through some personal transformations: growing into my new role as a father, the challenges of the COVID-19 pandemic, and job transitions. And while I was writing about this person who could go adrift without anyone knowing he was missing, I realized there had been a lot of steps in Hugh's life that led to him being *that* alone in the first place. I began working through his personal history, and in so doing, I realized that the text was allowing me to face some of my own personal fears: the fear of losing friends and family, the fear of losing a loved one and partner, the fear of falling short of the father I wanted to be for my kids. Hugh embodies all of those. So, in some ways, I was imagining how far I could fall and finding a way to voice my own fears through the experiences of this character.

Q: That brings me to process. Talk me through your approach to the writing of this book. How did it differ or align with your previous work?

A: I started *The Ice on the Lake* with little handwritten notes on the back of my daily calendar printout. At the time, I was feeling creatively stuck, like time was slipping by after *The Twenty-Ninth Day* came out. I knew I wanted to write another book, but I hadn't started it and didn't know what it should be. Then I had this inspiration of the story of a missing fisherman. I also had short snippets of time, just ten to fifteen minutes, when I could work on it. I'd look at the previous day's slip of paper to remind myself where I'd left off, and then I'd just start writing. That lowered the bar just enough for me to get going. I kept writing like that on the back of these sheets of printer paper for the first few chapters before I transcribed them and picked it up on the computer. In some ways that's similar to *The Twenty-Ninth Day*, which truly started as a journal, but it's also totally different writing fiction like *The Ice on the Lake*. After getting the bones of the novel's plot down, I worked on Hugh's personal backstory that would allow this totally secluded and hermitic old man to have someone who cares enough to notice he's missing in the first place. Things sort of fell into place as I worked through that, spoke with folks who provided input on the story, and did my own research. With all of my writing, I rely on the editing process to help that initial set of first drafts evolve into something that's so much better than how it started.

Q: In the original manuscript, Hugh came across as bitter, distant to his children, and friendless. In the final book, you give him a depth of character that makes him understandable, if not sympathetic. How hard was it to write his backstory so that he is now a relatable, redeemable, flawed person?

A: This was something I struggled with for a long time while writing the book. On the one hand, having him so unlikable made it obvious why he's alone and in this predicament, but on the other hand, it made it so no one cared about his situation—not the other characters in the book or the reader. I remember talking about this with my wife and saying,

"Why would anyone care that he's out there?" A big part of solving this challenge was getting into Hugh's mind, recognizing that things are not black and white. While he may be distant and cold, there was a process that led to him being that way, and multiple layers to his own experience and understanding of it. Recognizing that he's a person who overcame challenges and then fell from grace following personal tragedy made it easier to see how he evolved and devolved, how various situations would impact him, and how he'd respond. Some of that was internal dialogue and letting him voice his feelings. Some of that was action to show his capacity for kindness and for doing what seems like the wrong things (e.g., pushing his kids away) for altruistic reasons.

Q: In both your books, the reader is left with a sense of closure, but there isn't this sense of happily ever after. There's still a lot that is unsaid. Can you speak to that?

A: I think it's better to leave things up to the reader. For me, the essence of the story isn't how it ends; it's the momentum that it builds and then carries after the last page. Besides, we never know when something's truly over, so I think in a lot of ways it mirrors our own experience.